Heartwarming
Christmas Stories

Compiled by:

Marsha Hubler

ISBN: 0997197250
ISBN-13: 978-0-9971972-5-9

HEARTWARMING CHRISTMAS STORIES
Compiled by Marsha Hubler

Foreword

Christmas is always a special time of the year for Christians around the world. Remembering our Savior's birth renews within us our love and praise for the Lord Jesus Christ, who came to earth for the sole purpose of dying for our sins.

In this Christmas compilation, instead of writing my own stories, I invited six excellent authors to contribute to the heartwarming collection, promising to take the reader down the road of Christmas nostalgia.

Relax in your favorite chair with egg nog or a cappuccino and enjoy these stories that center around the birth of our Savior. And remember to keep the spirit of Christmas in your heart every day of the year!

Marsha

1 Cor. 15:10

www.marshahubler.com

Contents:

To Larry

On behalf of
the group!
Enjoy!
Love

About the Authors:

1. Edna Waidell Cravitz author of *One Special Christmas Charm*

When Edna Waidell Cravitz, retired elementary school teacher, isn't writing for children, you can find her kicking up her heels clog dancing (Yeehaw!), telling tales to children, and spending time with her family and two dogs, Rudy and Little Bear. Edna is delighted that her story "100 Things" was recently published in her favorite magazine, Highlights. Connect with her at www.ednawaidellcravitz.com.

2. Loree Lough author of *A Promise to Jake*

Bestselling author Loree Lough once sang for her supper, performing across the U.S. and Canada. Now and then, she blows the dust from her 6-string to croon a tune or two, but mostly, she writes novels that have earned hundreds of industry and "Readers' Choice" awards, 4- and 5-star reviews, and 7 book-to-movie options. Her 108th book, Guardians of the Heart, #3 in Whitaker's "Secrets on Sterling Street" historical series releases this November. Coming in early 2017, The Man She Knew, book #1 in her "By Way of the Lighthouse" series, is her 3rd for Harlequin Heartwarming.

3. Brenda K. Hendricks author of *Sly's Christmas Surprise*

Brenda K. Hendricks has had numerous short fiction stories and devotions published in compilations, as well as in periodicals. She has also written, illustrated, and published several children's picture books, a middle-grade novel, and two adult coloring books. All are available on Amazon. Connect with her at www.brendakhendricks.com.

4. Cindy O. Herman author of *Mrs. Fabersham's Secret Christmas Gift*

Freelance writer Cindy O. Herman won a Keystone Press Award for column writing and was featured in Erma Bombeck's HumorWriters.org for "Tractor Friends" (http://humorwriters.org/?s=Cindy+O.+Herman&submit=Search). Growing up with six siblings, she learned the importance of sharing and, sometimes, of having something all your own. Laugh with her at www.gigglesandgrinsblog.com.

5. Patti Souder author of *Hobby Horse Faith*

Enchanted by words and music, Patricia Souder has written, co-authored, or contributed to 14 published books and numerous plays, musicals, articles and children's stories. Co-host for Mailbag on WPEL, WPGM, and WBGM and former director of the Montrose Christian Writers Conference, Patti delights in meeting people in real life and Scripture. Check out her website at www.AlphaStarDrama.com.

6. Shirley Leonard author of *The Christmas Letters*

Shirley Leonard's devotionals in the *Secret Place*, the *Quiet Hour*, *Devotions*, and *Penned from the Heart* began her writing journey. Articles in *Women Alive, Pennsylvania,* and *American Window Cleaner* magazines and her first book, *With Each Passing Moment: Help and Hope for Caregivers* (Sonfire Media, 2012) continue the adventure.

Story One

One Special Christmas Charm

By Edna Waidell Cravitz

(A small Pennsylvania coal region town, early 1960s)

All the girls were wearing them. Bracelets. With charms dangling from them like gleaming ornaments on a Christmas tree. All gold and sparkly. An apple, a baby buggy, a ballerina, a four-leaf clover. Why, Kathy Lukas had an Eiffel Tower! Even if I had gotten just one charm, a special one, I would've been happy.

But no bracelet and no charm. Instead, I got a sweater and matching slacks, board games, pens and supplies for school, books—*well, I did like to read*—socks and even underwear. *Underwear! Who gets underwear for Christmas, for Heaven's sake?* I did get a new Flexible Flyer sled with bright red rails. A real beauty. Long enough to lie on face first and room enough to sit on with a friend.

Except I'd have to sit with my pain-in-the-neck kid brother. I suppose that's why I really got the sled in the first place. But I really wanted a bracelet. I was the only girl in the whole junior high school without one.

It was the worst Christmas ever.

And now here I was standing with my mother in front of the Presbyterian Church on Christmas morning at nine o'clock, trying to read some old paint-peeled sign. I had been to Midnight Mass at Saint Pete's the night before. Wasn't that enough? And I ached from tiredness from opening presents at six a.m.! This was the last place I wanted to be. And on top of that, three inches of snow covered the ground, the kind that was perfect for snowballs, and snow forts, and...sledding. Why, I could be racing that new sled right now this very minute. Even if I did have to sled with my eight-year-old pesky little brother. Some white Christmas this was.

I read the sign:

Community Soup Bowl

Open today 11:00 to 12:00

All welcome!

"Why are we here so early?" I asked. *After all, how long does it take to dish out some soup?* I had learned long ago what to say out loud and what to think inside.

"And why doesn't Mark Daniel have to be here?" *Now, that I decided to say out loud.*

I kicked some snow off my boots.

"The time will fly by," my mother said gently. "You'll like it; you'll see."

I gave her the roll-your-eyeballs no-I-will-NOT-like-it snooty face.

"And, your brother's too young," she added, ignoring my brazenness. And then she started to add, "And remember—"

"I know; I know. It's the little things in life that bring the greatest joy." I sighed. I sure wasn't feeling any joy at the moment standing here in front of the soup kitchen.

I moaned as I looked at my mother, her head showcasing that ridiculous white crocheted hat. Her Soup Bowl hat. It looked like a bunch of white miniature igloos stitched together. Scattered around the hat were some shiny spangles as big as nickels that shimmered and reflected the light. My mother looked like a walking rainbow. How could she embarrass me like that? *Get a new hat, Mom!*

We pulled open a heavy door and walked down a flight of creaky wooden steps that led to the basement of the church. A plain, drab room. At the front of the room was a stage; the curtains were pulled shut. An old, beat-up piano stood proudly by the side of the stage. At the back of the room was a kitchen where several men and women bustled about through a large rectangular window. I counted twelve long tables in the main part of the room. All of them still piled with chairs. I groaned.

A woman with the face of a saint dashed over to us.

11

"Welcome!" she said. She hugged my mother and turned to me. "You must be Margaret Mary."

"Maggie," I said. "My friends call me Maggie."

"I have heard so much about you, Maggie. I'm Mrs. Kelly."

There goes my mother again...talking about me to people I didn't even know.

"God bless you for helping today. We are expecting at least a hundred people."

A hundred!

She explained my job to me and then scurried off with my mother into the kitchen, their arms wrapped around each other's waist. My job was to get the tables ready *(no kidding!),* chat with the people, and serve chocolate milk.

The tables reminded me of the grab-bag sale at Nicholson's Five and Dime. If the customers didn't want the bargains, they'd just toss the merchandise back onto the tables any old which way. Except these tables were tossed with dozens of chairs that looked like a pile of tumbled-over brown dominoes. Now I had to untoss all the mixed-up chairs.

After setting up the chairs, I scrubbed the tables with a bleach solution. My hands smelled funny, kind of like the community swimming pool in the summer. Next, I decorated the tables with construction paper placemats and holiday greeting cards handmade by the Sunday school children. I had to admit, the artwork had taken my mind off charms and bracelets and sledding.

Pipe-smoking snowmen, manger scenes, bundled children, sleds, snow forts, reindeer, chubby Santas, and lots of glitter adorned the cards and placemats. They were brightly colored and definitely kid-made. Inside the cards were messages written by the little ones. They were irresistible

Dear Friend,

I hope Santa comes to your house for Christmas. But you better tell him NOT to come down the chimney because he is too F-A-T, FAT!!! He eats too many creme puffs from Keenan's Bakery. He might get stuck. Leave a note and tell him to come in the front door. Then he can put the presents by your tree. Be sure you only open the presents with *your* name on them because you do not want to open your brother's and get something dumb like a football.

Love, Your friend,

Sandy

PS You can put out carrots AND cookies for Rudolph. He is *not* too fat.

*****

Dear Friend,

I hope you get a lot of presents from Santa. We put out cookies for Santa, but my brother licks them. Do you get presents for Christmas? Do you need a new car? We need a new car because my mother backed the car out of the garage. She forgot to put up the door. We need a new door, too. My dad was mad. He said it was a good thing that Santa drove a sleigh. Then he didn't have to worry about Mrs. Claus backing it out of the garage. My mother cried. I had to walk to school. Our Sunday school teacher told us to wish you a Merry Christmas and a Happy New Year!

Love,

Christopher Michael James

*****

Mother interrupted my card reading when she came to help me place tissue-paper flowers on the tables. Kid-made, of course. Red, blue, pink, yellow, orange, green. A kaleidoscope of colors. The tables looked like they were scattered with accordion-winged butterflies. Butterflies in winter!

Beautiful! Just beautiful.

A sense of pride flushed through me.

At exactly 10:30, not 11:00 like the sign read, but 10:30, a stream of people started coming down the creaky stairs. Slowly. Like molasses in January, my mother would say. Men, women. Old people, not so old people. Heavy people. Skinny people. Regular-

14

looking people. Worn-out looking people. A man in a plaid shirt, no coat. A woman with a bright red babushka. A young mother with two boys. A man with a little girl.

Two boys and a little girl!

"Mother!" I cried. "Children come to the soup kitchen?"

"Times are tough," was all my mother said.

I had never really believed that some children didn't have enough food. Suddenly the food on my supper table was looking pretty good. Maybe all those stories about starving children were true. *I better clean my plate the next time we have those stuffed peppers.*

Most of the people went straight to the coffee table and poured themselves a cup. Some went directly to a chair. Some talked to the helpers. You could tell they were regulars.

Women fussed over the tissue paper flowers. The red babushka lady decorated her vest with them, poking the pipe cleaner stems through the vest's button holes. "Look how they match my clothes," she laughed. She was delightful.

I laughed right along with her. It amazed me at how she could find such joy in something so little.

Quickly gathering up some of the flowers, I twisted them together. I handed each child a bouquet. The children clapped their hands and squealed with joy. You would have thought they had won the grand-prize stuffed animal at the annual fireman's block party.

The creaking stairs suddenly grabbed my attention. A man with a wooden cane came hobbling down. Why it was Old Man Higgins! I had seen him a hundred times before. He would walk up and down the streets searching for soda bottles to cash in for a nickel each.

He made a beeline for my mother and grabbed her hand. "God bless you, Mary McRooney. How have you been?" he said vigorously shaking her hand.

My mother knows Mr. Higgins?

"I'm just fine, Mr. Higgins," replied my mother.

"Oh, call me George," said Mr. Higgins. "I'm not your teacher anymore!" He chuckled and headed for the hot coffee.

My mouth dropped open like a hungry steam shovel scooping up gravel.

"Mr. Higgins was your teacher!" I almost shouted the words.

"He was my teacher in the fourth grade. Best teacher I ever had." Mom looked at Mr. Higgins, her eyes filled with admiration.

"What is he doing here at the Soup Bowl?"

"Came upon some hard times, I guess."

Together we watched the old man pour his coffee.

I thought about the way the neighborhood bullies treated Mr. Higgins when he was collecting soda bottles. I would just stand there and watch. A confession and an act of contrition were trying to burst out of my body, so I just started babbling.

16

"Mom, the Thompson twins make fun of old…I mean…Mr. Higgins. They call him hibble-hobble Higgins because he walks with a limp. They throw soda bottle caps at him."

My mother grimaced.

Witnessing the bullying was not a pretty sight. I never joined in, but I had never done anything about it either. I just stood back and watched the bullies. *Shame on me.* Now I was pretty sure that that was the wrong thing to do. No, I *knew* it was the wrong thing. Just thinking about doing something wrong was a sin, so I couldn't imagine how bad it was to watch something bad and not do anything about it. My mind was already formulating my words for next Saturday afternoon's confession to Father Anthony.

I couldn't stop looking at Mr. Higgins. He was chatting with the plaid-shirt man. Maybe Mr. Higgins was just plain lonely. The pride that filled me a few minutes ago drained right out of me like swirling bathtub water going down the pipe.

"Attention!" called Mrs. Kelly. "The meal is ready. Please bow your heads."

"Dear Heavenly Father, thank you for blessing us with this food today, for bringing us all together on this glorious Christmas morning, and thank you for our volunteers. Amen."

An echo of "amens" filled the room.

My mother blessed herself, kissed her rosary, and slipped it back into her pocket. I blessed myself, too, and said a little prayer to God, thanking him for the food that would be on my table when I got home, and then I whispered a little P.S.: "Dear God, from now on I will be more grateful for the things I have, even my little brother. Amen."

A volunteer called a table number and each matching table group lined up at the kitchen window to get their meals. The rest jibber-jabbered and waited patiently.

Meat loaf, rice, corn, and a sugar cookie shaped like a tree sprinkled with bright green sugar crystals. That's what the meal was. *Meat loaf*...on Christmas day! Well. At least it wasn't soup, and the cookies were from Keenan's bakery.

Why, I could just smell the aroma of our fresh turkey and sage stuffing mother had already prepared and was now cooking in our oven. Dad was the guardian of the turkey as he waited for us to return home. He and my brother were probably right now fixing Dad's famous gravy.

Nope. No turkey. But not one person complained. Seems the only one complaining this Christmas morning was me.

As the people waited their turns, piano music filled the room like a sweet fragrance. I turned and looked. It was Mr. Higgins! He played beautifully. One Christmas carol after the other. The plaid-shirt man got up and started singing. His voice was as powerful as a professional singing "The Star Spangled Banner" at a baseball game. Soon everyone was singing:

"Joy to the world! the Lord has come;

Let Earth receive her king...."

I couldn't help but sing myself, and I really belted it out too.

"Come on, Kate Smith," my mother said with a grin. *How she loved that singer's magnificent voice.* "Time to serve the milk." By now everyone had been served their meat loaf dinner.

My mother and I began pouring milk. I loved serving the chocolate. It was the all-time favorite. I couldn't believe that something like chocolate milk could make people so happy.

As we served, a small, frail elderly woman handed a paper bag to my mother.

"For you," she said to my mother, her wrinkled face glowing with pride.

My mother opened the bag and pulled out a white crocheted scarf. Why, it looked just like my mother's hat. The same bumpy miniature igloos. *So that's where my mother got that funny-looking crocheted hat!* I noticed the woman's hands. They were gnarled with arthritis. It must have taken her weeks to crochet that scarf! A lump as big as an apple grew in my throat.

"Oh, Frances," said my mother, "it's beautiful!" She wrapped the scarf around her neck and posed like a famous movie star. They hugged. No words were said out loud, but at that moment, thousands of words had passed between the two women. A deep and profound respect for my mother and the elderly lady flooded my entire being. Not to mention the goose bumps that went up and down my arms.

"And I'll have chocolate!" Frances suddenly cried. We all laughed. I'm not quite sure why, but it sure did make the situation better. I poured her a glass of chocolate milk right up to the tippy top of the rim.

Next we poured milk for the two little boys. They must have been brothers because they sure did look alike. One wanted chocolate, and one wanted white. I thought that was kind of funny. I thought all kids liked chocolate milk; it was like having a candy bar in liquid form.

"You're next!" I said to the little girl. "Chocolate or white?"

"Chocolate!" cried the little girl, reaching her skinny little arms up into the air. She was as cute as a doll. Curly red hair, big hazel eyes, and a smile that melted your heart like butter on a hot waffle. She looked like an angel. Even though it was warm inside, she was still wearing a pink hat and scarf. A pair of matching mittens was neatly placed by her plate. All hand crocheted.

"Did you have a nice Christmas?" I asked the little girl as I poured the chocolate milk, right up to the top, of course.

"Oh, yes," said the girl. "Santa brought me presents. He brought me my hat and scarf! And my mittens, too." She quickly put on the tiny mittens and started clapping.

"And Daddy and I went to church this morning, she continued. "Reverend Miller gave me a present too. Look!"

She opened a tiny box. Inside was a small wooden hand-carved baby Jesus. He was wrapped in a blanket lying in a cradle.

"I'll keep him with me all the time," she said kissing the tiny infant. "When I say my prayers at night, the Baby Jesus will be right there with me. We'll pray to my mommy because my mommy is in Heaven with the real Baby Jesus."

My breath caught in my throat like a penny jammed in a gumball machine. I just couldn't get it out. The elation I felt a few minutes ago crashed like a tumbling house of cards.

"Mom!" I finally managed to squeak out. I felt desperate. I couldn't say anything more. The words were all choked up inside of me. My mother gave me a quick look and a little shake of her head.

"Tuberculosis," she whispered. *Tuberculosis! My own grandfather had died from TB.* I remembered the test we had to take to make sure our lungs weren't sick too. I wondered if the little girl had to get her wrist prickled and then have the doctor look for the tell-tale bumps.

My mother knew what I was thinking. "She's fine," she said. Her mother died years ago when she was just a baby. The father fell apart. Lost his job."

The little girl picked up her glass and drank half of it. I filled it right back up.

"Oh, boy!" The little girl looked straight at me. Her smile could warm a polar bear's nose. "Santa brought me gloves and a hat and mittens, Reverend Miller gave me Baby Jesus, and now you're giving me chocolate milk."

She slurped some more milk, licked her chocolate moustache, and threw her arms around me.

"This is the best Christmas ever!" she proclaimed.

The flood gates poured open and filled my body with more shame than could fill the Grand Canyon. I squeezed my eyes to hold back the pools of tears, but maybe, just maybe I was really trying to hold back the selfish images of me. Me being brazen. Me not appreciating what I had. Me about to have a feast of turkey and stuffing and cranberry sauce and homemade pumpkin pie. Me wishing for a silly charm bracelet when this little girl didn't even have a mother. Me not even asking my own mother why she wore the white hat or why she came to the Community Soup Bowl every Saturday.

I hugged that little girl as hard as I could. Maybe I could squeeze some of that little angel's goodness right into me. Me, Margaret Mary McRooney. The only girl in the whole junior high school who didn't have a charm bracelet—or any sense of what was really important in life.

After that, I just kept filling glasses. Somehow pouring the milk just let out all of the crazy mixed-up feelings that were popping around inside my body.

"What's your name?" I asked the little girl.

"Lily. Like the flower. Daddy says that flowers bring people great joy."

I couldn't have thought of a better name for the little cherub, except maybe—Angel.

By now, people were starting to leave the soup kitchen.

"Come on, Maggie," interrupted my mother. "We have to help at the canned goods table."

Lily gave me a good-bye-see-ya-later smile, and I headed over to a long table at the side of the room.

The table was filled with brown paper bags. The kind you get at the grocery store. Each bag contained three cans of food— one soup, one vegetable, one fruit— and a long loaf of square white bread. As the people left, each one received a bag. I felt like Santa Claus, or rather Mrs. Claus, giving out more gifts. *Except there should have at least been a jar of peanut butter to go along with that white bread.*

"Merry Christmas!" I said quite cheerily as I passed out the bags. I noticed that the red babushka lady had a handful of flowers, cards, and placemats. "To decorate my house for Christmas!" she cried. Our house was decorated with a real Christmas tree complete with glass ornaments and sparkling tinsel. I looked at my mother. She was smiling even though her eyes glistened with tears.

Finally, Mr. Higgins struggled through the line. He could barely walk, let alone carry his bag at the same time.

"Come on," said my mother. "We'll help Mr. Higgins take his bag home. He just lives down the street."

"No," I said. "You stay here. I'll help walk Mr. Higgins down the street and see that he gets to his door."

It seemed to take forever to get Mr. Higgins up the steps. When we finally got outside, the sight took our breath away. It had snowed the whole time we were in the soup kitchen. Huge snowflakes were still gently tumbling to the ground. I loved how they fell on my eyelashes. I caught some with my tongue. Mr. Higgins chuckled.

The snow glistened on the sidewalks, streets, cars, and trees. Children's laughter echoed through the cold air. It sounded like some boys were having a snowball fight in the town park across the street.

With one arm, I held onto the grocery bag. With the other, I guided Mr. Higgins by his elbow. I clenched my teeth as we trekked along the snow-packed sidewalk. It was an accident waiting to happen. We maneuvered slowly down the street.

We certainly don't want any broken hips, especially not on Christmas day.

As we walked, something zinged right past the side of my face. It sprayed little jabs of ice into my cheeks. *Thud!* Something smacked me square in the back. *Swish!* Another something zipped right by Mr. Higgins's face.

Turning around was not the best idea I ever had, but I went and did it anyway.

Pow! A snowball exploded right on my chest.

24

It was the Thompson twins! Billy and Bobby! And they were pelting us with snowballs.

"Look who it is," cried Billy as he whipped another ball of ice at us. "It's Maggie McRooney, and look who's her buddy! Hibble-Hobble Higgins!" Soon they were throwing piles of snow at us. Mr. Higgins turned as white as the snow-blanketed streets.

"Stop it!" I cried. "Stop it!" I wasn't very good at defending myself, let alone Mr. Higgins.

"What's the matter with you helping that old bum?" said Bobby. "Are you nuts or something?"

"Yeah, that's it," said Billy. "She's just plum crazy. Maybe we should wrap her up and put her in the loony bin!"

"Yeah, let's put Maggie McRooney in the *loony* bin!"

"Loony McRooney! Loony McRooney!" They chanted over and over. Their evilness turned my stomach, and their words hurt like splinters poking my insides.

"Just keep walking," said Mr. Higgins.

But they kept after us like a pack of wild animals after their prey. Only they were chanting and kicking snow instead of growling and stalking.

Suddenly, Mr. Higgins's feet slid right out from under him and down he went. *Thud!*

My heart just about pounded through my chest.

The two cowards stopped dead in their tracks, turned, and ran. I saw Billy Thompson fall right on his backside, knocking over his brother on the way down.

Good! That's what you get for being mean to an old man.

I helped Mr. Higgins to his feet and brushed off the thick layer of snow stuck to his coat.

"Oh, Mr. Higgins," I cried still brushing his coat as the bag of goods slipped from my arm. "Are you all right?"

Mr. Higgins looked a bit stunned. I chomped on my lower lip waiting for him to answer.

"Oh, dear," he finally said.

"What is it, Mr. Higgins?" my voice quivered. "Should I run get my mother?"

The few moments he took to respond felt like hours slowly ticking on a watched clock. Finally he lifted his arms and started gently flapping them up and down.

Oh, no! He must have hit his head! Old Mr. Higgins has lost his mind!

"Missed my chance to make a snow angel when I was down there," he said quite seriously.

Laughter popped out of us like hot popcorn flying out of a pot.

"I'm just fine, child," said Mr. Higgins picking up his cane. "That six inches of snow cushioned my fall like a soft, fluffy blanket."

The chinker chain clicked the light bulb on in our heads as we thought the same thing at the same time. We just looked at each other, plopped down in the snow, and started waving our arms wildly across the white fluff. Now *our* laughter was echoing across the town. *Who ever thought making a snow angel could be so much fun?*

After flailing in the snow and then admiring our winged wonders for a few minutes, I grabbed the soggy grocery bag and delivered Mr. Higgins to the front door of his building. His apartment just happened to be on top of Keenan's Bakery. *How lucky was that!* I waved good-bye and started back for the Soup Bowl. As I headed back, I marveled at how Mr. Higgins had not said one unkind word about the Thompson twins.

When I got back to the Presbyterian Church, my mother was waiting for me by the paint-peeled sign. I told her about Mr. Higgins and the Thompson twins and the snow angels. And then I just wrapped my arms around my mother and hugged her.

My mother pulled a little brown lunch bag out of her pocket and handed it to me.

"What's this?" I asked.

"Oh, just a little something I was saving for a special occasion. Like now. It's your favorite sandwich. Open it."

No way! There's no sandwich inside this bag. I could feel my heart pitter-patter as I opened the bag. Inside was a tiny box wrapped in shimmering red paper tied with silver ribbon. My heart flipped like

27

an Olympic gymnast. I carefully tore off the paper and opened the lid of the box. The shiny gold caught my eye.

"Oh, Mother!" I cried as I hugged her again.

"You'll just have to wait until your birthday for the bracelet," she said.

I suddenly turned and started running for the steps to the basement of the church.

"Where are you going?" my mother asked.

"I'm going to see Lily," I cried as I started down the steps.

"She's gone," she said.

"What!" I just could not believe that Lily was gone.

"She left a few minutes ago with her father. They headed down Broad Street. Hurry!" Somehow my mother knew what I was up to.

I flew back up those basement steps and started running down Broad Street right in the middle of the road. Slush and snow splashed everywhere. I didn't see Lily and her father. I stopped at the corner and looked down Market Street. No Lily. I ran to the end of the next block and looked down Spruce Street. Nothing. And then I saw it. A little pink hat bobbing up and down.

"Lily!" I cried. Legs aching from running in the heavy snow, I still kept running.

"Lily," I said as soon as I caught up to her. "I have something for you." Huffing and puffing, I handed Lily the box.

She took off the lid. Her eyes lit up like stars in the sky.

"Look, Daddy, look!" she cried, "An angel!" Her tiny hands took the angel from the box. She held it to her cheek.

"It's a special charm for a special little girl," I said.

"Oh, Daddy!" Lily cried. "This *is* the best Christmas ever!"

Lily wrapped her arms around me, and her hug filled me with warmth I knew would last me the whole winter. It was better than the warm feeling you get from a hot cup of steaming cocoa.

She took her daddy's hand and started to leave, and then suddenly she turned, ran back, and grabbed me. She kept patting my sides like I was a drum. I giggled.

"Come on now, Lily," said her father, "time to go." He nodded a thank you to me and took Lily by the hand. I stood there and watched them walk down the street until I could no longer see the pink bobbing hat.

*****

Mom was waiting for me when I finally got home. As soon as I walked through the door, I told my father and my brother all about my day. I couldn't stop talking.

I was still wearing my coat when my father finally said, "Maggie, dear, why don't you take off your coat and stay for a while?"

I laughed. As I took off my coat, something tumbled out of my pocket. I leaned over and gently picked up the object. "Oh,

29

Lily," I whispered. I cradled it in my hands and held it to my cheek. Then I ran upstairs and tucked it under my pillow.

When I came back down, I joined my family at the kitchen table.

"Bow your heads for grace," said my father. "In the name of the Father, the Son, and the Holy Ghost." We all blessed ourselves and together recited the prayer, "Bless us, O Lord, and these Thy gifts, which we are about to receive from Thy bounty, through Christ our Lord. Amen."

And then the feast began. We had turkey and stuffing and cranberry sauce, Dad's famous gravy, of course, and homemade pumpkin pie topped with real whipped cream.

*****

Joy to the World! The Lord has come! The words floated in my head as I fluffed up my pillow. I said my prayers, and settled in for the night. In my heart was a new-found spirit filled with joy given to me by an old man and a five-year-old little girl. A girl named Lily—*my* special sparkling charm.

I couldn't wait to go back to the Community Soup Bowl with my mother to see Lily, Mr. Higgins, the plaid shirt man, the babushka lady—all of them. Life was good.

As I drifted off to sleep a knock on the door interrupted my reverie.

"Maggie…." my mother started.

"I know; I know," I said excitedly as I sat straight up. "It's the little things in life that bring the greatest joy. Like chocolate milk and snow angels and a funny crocheted hat. Like a little wooden carving of the Baby Jesus. Like Old Man Higgins and a little angel named Lily."

"Maggie," my mother said. "I'm so very proud of you."

My mother kissed me good-night and clicked off the light. "Merry Christmas," she said as she closed the door.

"Merry Christmas, Mom."

I rolled onto my side and closed my eyes. I took great comfort knowing that under my pillow was a tiny carved Baby Jesus watching over me on this glorious day. And I knew that he was watching over Lily, too.

It *was* the best Christmas ever.

A Promise to Jake

By Loree Lough

Cradling the phone between chin and shoulder, Homer O'Tuathail used one hand to tear a speaking invitation from the fax machine, deleted an e-mail message with the other. "Hold on, Bobby," he muttered into the mouthpiece, "now the doorbell is ringing."

"You have a portable. I'll talk, you walk."

Chuckling, Homer shoved back from the desk and headed for the foyer. "Better be careful, 'cause you know what they say...."

"What who says?"

"The sages. The powers that be. The wise men: 'All work and no play turns nice-guy literary agents into slave drivers.'"

"If I was a nice guy, who'd whip you into shape?" Bobby asked, laughing. "So who's ringing your bell at the dinner hour?"

Homer opened the door in time to see the brown delivery truck pulling away from the circular drive. "UPS," he answered, retrieving a small package from the marble bench beside the door, "and the sticker on the box says 'Do Not Open 'Til Christmas', just like in the movies."

Bobby sighed. "And so the rich get richer. Presents come from out of the blue to the man who already has everything."

Homer snorted good-naturedly and headed inside. "Yeah. Right. Everything…except time." He kicked the door shut and read "Knoxville" on the return address label. Who did he know in Tennessee? Jake Donnelly used to live near Gatlinburg, but last Homer heard, he'd moved to Dallas.

Jake.

No matter how many months passed between conversations, Jake, with his slow southern drawl and feet-on-the-ground logic, was an island of sanity in Homer's frenetic world. How long since they'd last talked? Five years? Six? Lately, it seemed his life had spun out of control. Maybe all he needed was a 'Jake fix' to get a handle on things. Homer made a mental note to give his old pal a call, soon as Bobby hung up.

"So what's in the box?"

Homer gave it a cursory glance. "Don't know. Don't care. Only thing I'm interested in right now is a good night's sleep. Hate to be rude, but I've been up thirty-six straight hours. Can you cut to the chase, tell me why you're calling?"

"You're going to New York. Red-eye flight, tonight. Reserved you a suite at the Sheraton, walking distance from—"

"You're not serious."

"As a heart attack."

Homer drove a hand through his hair. "What's so all-fired important it can't wait until after the first of the year?"

"Schweetheart," came the terrible Bogart imitation, "ish Letterman important enough for ya?"

Bobby had the 'schmooze' part of agenting down pat. And the lingo part, too. But wait a minute. Had he said Letterman?

Ever since Homer's first best-seller, decades ago, Bobby had succeeded in booking Homer on all the major late night talk shows. All but Letterman, that is. "Whose feet do I have to kiss to make that happen?"

Bobby laughed. "Only mine, Homer m'boy, only mine. And speaking of feet, get yours moving or you'll miss your flight."

He groaned. "You know how I feel about last-minute stuff."

"Oh, quit whining. This is the opportunity of a lifetime. You're a last-minute replacement for Zac Efron on tomorrow's show. The network has been airing commercials all week, and you know what that means...."

It meant nearly every female over thirteen would tune in for a glimpse of their favorite Hollywood heartthrob. "'And market studies show that women buy most of the books sold in the U.S.,'" Homer said, quoting the agent.

"Nice to know somebody listens when I talk. Now hear this: I spared you the pre-interview nonsense by emailing your bio to Letterman's people."

Homer was about to ask why Zac cancelled when Bobby added, "By the way, your flight takes off at eleven."

"Aw for the luvva Pete," he said, glancing at his Rolex. "I have two hours to pack and get to BWI?"

"A literary genius and a math wiz to boot. Maybe I'll call you Einstein from now on. Sure beats that moniker your mama gave you."

Homer growled under his breath. In the early days, he and Bobby had gone round and round on the subject, but Homer held his ground: His name was all his parents had left him; he'd go back to being a short-order cook rather than change it. In the end, Bobby gave in. "I guess if a goofy name could work for that old-time singer, Engleburt," he'd said, "it can work for you." And he began parlaying Homer's rugged good looks with his less-than-sexy name.

It had been a wise choice, signing with Bobby Barnes, but like everything else about his fast-lane life, certain negatives couldn't be avoided. "You know how I feel about last-minute trips," he repeated.

"But Homer. Picture it. Letterman, hawking your latest book-turned-screenplay. It'll be the next box office hit, I tell you!"

Homer got the picture, all right, and he had to admit, he liked what he saw. "Still—"

"Don't worry, hot shot, you're going first class all the way, as usual. Just don't let the pomp and circumstance bloat your brain."

"What're the chances I'll get a fat head," Homer said, chuckling, "with you running around, pin in hand?"

Bobby's laughter crackled through the line.

"Hang up, you greedy schmuck. I have a lot to do if I'm going to make that fligh—"

"Oh, cry me a river why don't you. Besides, if I know you, your suitcase hasn't been opened since you got back from L.A. last week."

Homer grinned, knowing that 'packing' would require little more than replacing the dirty underclothes in his overnight bag with clean ones. "You know me too well, pal."

"That's why you pay me the big bucks, schweetheart."

Homer exhaled. "I have a good mind to cancel this red-eye, book a flight for first thing in the morni—"

Bobby resumed his Bogart imitation: "You don't get on that plane, you'll regret it. Maybe not now, maybe not tomorrow, but shoon, and for the resht of your life."

Homer chuckled. "You can be such a jerk."

"Yeah, but thanks to you, I'm a rich jerk. Now go pack, or I'll sharpen my pin."

Homer hung up and radioed the garage, and while waiting for his driver to fire up the Jaguar, he turned off lights, shut down the computer, and locked up. He could have done it all in one-tenth the time if he'd trade this ridiculous McMansion for his little cabin in Buckley, West Virginia. The area reminded him of Ireland, and much as he loved the place, getting into and out of the Yew Mountains wasn't quick or convenient. So for now, he'd live here, and spend his free time there.

The Jaguar's horn blared, and Homer hurried into the front hall. He'd just finished keying in the alarm code when he noticed the package from Tennessee on the foyer table. Tucking it under his arm, he booted the suitcase onto the porch and slammed the front door.

"'Evenin', Homer," his driver said.

"'Evenin', Sam. Sorry to bother you at this hour."

Grinning, Sam shrugged. "Hey. That's what you pay me the big bucks for."

Word-for-word what Bobby had said, moments earlier. Homer could only shake his head. After this gig, he intended to see exactly how many people he was paying 'the big bucks'.

As the sleek sedan purred down I-95 between Homer's estate and Baltimore's airport, he fielded half a dozen calls on his cell phone: Bobby, informing Homer that Letterman would send a car to meet him at Kennedy International; a Letterman staffer, fact-checking the emailed bio; Homer's editor:

"Congratulations, ladies' man," she complained. "You made the cover of People. Again. I'm beginning to think you like being known as—wait, let me quote the headline—'The Silver Fox of the Literary World'."

He'd long suspected the young woman had a crush on him, so Homer soft-pedaled his response. "Of course I don't like it," he admitted. "Why would I like being reminded I'm sixty-four years old, in a decade when—"

"Then why," she interrupted, "do you insist on hanging around with all those...with all those floozies!"

"Floozies?" He laughed. "You're not old enough to use language like that, young lady!"

"Very funny, big shot."

He ignored her sarcasm. "It's publicity, Lorna. Shameless self-promotion and nothing more." Not the whole truth, but not exactly a lie, either. "Those tabloid stories are great for book sales. Just ask my agent."

"Oh, give me a break. Like I'd get a straight answer from a man who's been cheating on his wife since his wedding night. No wonder you guys get along so well. You're two of a kind."

Frowning, Homer considered reminding her that he'd never been married. Instead, he pressed the phone's 'end' button. His publisher wasn't paying him nearly enough to put up with guff from an editor young enough to be his granddaughter.

Fifteen minutes later, slouching in a bucket-shaped black chair at Gate C-19, his phone chirped again. Scowling, Homer turned it off and dropped it into his shirt pocket. "Thank God for voice mail," he muttered, grabbing the package from Tennessee.

As its plain brown wrapper slid unnoticed to the floor, Homer stared at the faded Buster Brown shoebox. How long since he'd seen it? Thirty-nine, forty years? He'd worked hard to keep everything about Dexter Domicile buried deep in his memory. Now, as if thumbing through a deck of cards, pictures of the orphanage and the children who'd called it home flashed in his mind. Of the dozens who promised to stay in touch after leaving Dexter, only one had...

...and that one kept his most cherished belonging in a box just like this.

Homer read the hand-written note taped to the lid. "You always seemed to know what was important. That's why I'm counting on you to take care of this for me." And it was signed, "Jake."

His mouth went dry and his ears grew hot when he lifted the cover. "Oh, God," he prayed, closing his eyes. 'Don't let it be...let it be anything but—"

When he opened his eyes, Homer saw a golden wing tip, partially hidden beneath a layer of wrinkled white tissue. Hands trembling and heart knocking, Homer admitted what it meant:

Jake was dead. He never would have parted with the angel for any other reason.

Tears pooled in the corners of Homer's eyes as an announcement warbled from the overhead speaker. "Ladies and gentlemen, we at United would like to welcome our passengers to flight number 2537. We'll board in just a few minutes and—"

Homer inhaled a shaky breath as a whirl of questions swam in his head. Had accident or illness ended the life of his old friend? Had Jake suffered, or had a merciful God taken him quickly? Had he been alone, or with friends when…

Friends.

The word no sooner formed in Homer's mind than a condemning thought followed: If you'd been a real friend to Jake, you'd know the answers.

Well, his intentions had been good. Every year, like clockwork, he'd typed reminders into his daily planner: "Call Jake" on a January page. "Drop note to Jake" in June. "Jake's b-day" every August, and "Send Jake's Christmas card" in December.

But a deadline or a book signing or an invitation to speak at a writers' conference always got in the way. He could excuse the work-related business that interfered with staying in touch, but it wasn't so easy admitting that more often than not, monkey business had been to blame.

He'd figured there'd always be time to reconnect with Jake, tomorrow, next week, in a month or two…. Because what man in his right mind would pass up an opportunity to woo willing young groupies and writer wanna-bees? Not the Silver Fox! he thought, grimacing. "Yeah, Homer," he said, disgusted with himself, "you're all man, all right."

The overhead voice interrupted his thoughts again: "We are now ready to begin boarding our first class passengers."

But Homer barely heard it. He was too busy thinking about how foolishly he'd spent his time…and lived his life. Slump-shouldered, he hung his head. Throat aching from trying to choke back his shame, he looked at Jake's angel, whose satin dress was now more yellow than white. The gold that once gleamed from her halo and wingtips had all but disappeared. At least the tiny pink mouth still curved up in a gentle smile, and painted-on black lashes still framed blue eyes.

The image of Jake, telling the story of how the angel had come to be his, flared in Homer's memory. He'd seemed so scrawny, such an easy mark, sitting cross-legged in the middle of his lumpy mattress that Christmas Eve so many years ago. But Homer and the other boys in Donaldson's Dormitory learned soon enough that although Jake was smaller than other kids his age, he was anything but defenseless….

Slapping a hand to the back of his neck, Homer took a gulp of air and ignored the reservations clerk: "Passengers seated in rows 30 through 25 may now begin boarding."

For some reason, he thought of the brand-new, hand-blown bowl in his living room. He'd shelled out several thousand bucks for it because his decorator said it would match the bookends on his mantle. Days ago, while propping his size thirteen Italian loafers onto the coffee table, he'd chipped the one-of-a-kind vessel...and shrugged it off. Jake's angel probably hadn't cost a dollar, brand new, yet he'd lovingly cared for it for half a century. The contrasts were obvious, and shamed Homer further.

Gently, he covered the angel with wrinkly tissue, replaced the lid, and eased the box into his carry-on as a scheme took shape in his head:

He was not going to New York. He had more important things to do.

He left a voice mail message for Bobby; the agent deserved as much lead time as possible to line up another client for the Letterman show. Too impatient to wait for Sam to make the return trip to BWI, Homer flagged a taxi and rattled off his address. "Know any place that sells Christmas trees between here and there?"

"The day before Christmas Eve?" The cabbie met Homer's eyes in the rearview mirror. "I guess."

"Stop there first, then." He noticed a corner of the Buster Brown box, poking from his unzipped carry-on. "You always seemed to know what's important," Jake had written. Back at Dexter, that might have been true, but somewhere along the way....

"Pickin's are liable to be slim, though," the driver said, "'cause it's kinda late to be buyin' a tree."

He knuckled his eyes, shook his head. "Kinda late for a lot of things," he said, mostly to himself.

But maybe, Homer thought, ignoring the driver's indifferent shrug, with Jake's angel to remind him what 'worthwhile' really meant, it wasn't too late to salvage a shred, at least, of the man he used to be.

*****

The cabbie had frowned as Homer laid the scraggly pine atop the spare tire. "You didn't pay good money for it, I hope."

Was there such a thing as 'good money,' he wondered? Homer didn't think so.

Now, the poor lop-sided pine stood beside Homer's desk, leaning slightly left under the weight of gold ornaments and white lights. The haunting voice of James Taylor crooned from the stereo: "...but I always thought I'd see you one more time again...."

The lyrics echoed in his head. How many chances had he blown? Dozens. Hundreds. And for what? To sell a few more books? For wine-and-dine time with women whose IQs wouldn't match his age, even on their best days?

Homer caught a glimpse of himself in the chromed finish of his reading lamp. Looks like you caught that red-eye after all, he told himself, swiping at a silvery tear tracking down his cheeks.

He straightened the angel. Jake wouldn't believe how much the tree looked like the one they snuck into Dexter the night when—

The telephone jangled. Again. Frustrated by its constant intrusion, Homer yanked the cord from the wall. "Thank God for voice mail," he repeated, dropping heavily onto the seat of his desk chair. Cracking his knuckles and working the kinks from his neck, he hunched over his computer's keyboard. There had to be a way to give meaning to Jake's death, to his life. Homer didn't know any other way, except with words.

He'd wanted to tell this story since his first book hit the stands twenty-five years ago. This one probably wouldn't make the best-seller list, as his private eye series had. Likely wouldn't earn movie options, either, the way his cop books did. He didn't believe in throwing his weight around, but this time, he'd do whatever it took to get the story into print. He owed Jake that much.

He stared at the blinking cursor. "I've let you down big time, Jake," he said, eyes on the blank white screen. Maybe telling his friend's story would ease his conscience. Squaring his shoulders, Homer pulled out the keyboard drawer and gave his knuckles one last crack, and began to type:

Jake's Angel

by Homer O'Tuathail

It was me who dubbed the new arrivals 'rookies', because Lord, they had a lot to learn! Didn't matter if they came to Dexter Domicile for Displaced Juveniles wearing store-bought shoes or no shoes at all, or if they carried their belongings in a valise or a flour sack. They all climbed those red-brick stairs in one of two ways: Crying out loud, or silent and stiff as a cemetery angel. Usually, they were handed over by guilty-faced relatives who said things like, "If only there was another way..." and "When things get better, we'll be back for you...."

A rooky showed up one Christmas Eve, a tattered name tag hanging around his neck and a beat-up Buster Brown shoebox under one arm. He didn't seem to notice that the sole of his left shoe flapped when he walked. If he knew there was a hole in the right knee of his threadbare trousers, or that the frayed sleeves of his jacket ended inches above his wrists, he hid it well. And if it bothered him that Miss Germane all but shoved him up the walk, well, you couldn't tell by looking at him. The most memorable thing about him, right off the bat, was that way he had of smiling with his whole body. It started with blue eyes that crinkled at the corners, and ended with a hop-step on those time-worn shoes.

Half-way up the flagstone path, he stopped dead in his tracks and whipped the old gray cap from his head. Using it as a visor, he glanced up at Dexter's windows. I watched his lips move as he counted to himself: One, two, three...eighteen, nineteen, twenty.... "Wow," he whispered, "who's in charge of polishin' all that glass?" Then he blinked a few times and did a neat about-face that would have put any soldier to shame. "Ma'am," he said to Miss Germane, "my Aunt Cassie, she said I'd be sleepin' in a dorm'tory with other boys. Is that true?"

Nodding, she gave her best thin-lipped smile.

"How many young'uns you got in this place?"

"Three hundred and five," she said, like she was proud of the number.

"Countin' me?"

"Counting you."

"Shoo-eee. That's a lot of orphans." He shook his head. "I don't spoze new kids get top digs." Looking from Miss Germane's puzzled face to mine and back again, he explained: "Way I see it, the high floors is fu'thest from the wood stove in winter, an' even a simpleton knows heat rises in summer." Bobbing his head, he added, "Reckon a boy would hafta be some kinda big shot to get a bed down on a low floor in a place this big."

Miss Germane's mouth dropped open, and I'd never seen her cheeks any redder than that, not even when Jimmy Stoker described for her entire science class exactly how babies were made, right down to pictures on the chalkboard.

"I'm not sure which dormitory floor you'll be assigned to, Mr. Donnelly," she said, nose in the air.

With his thumb, the rookie pointed at me. "Will this boy, here, be in my dormitory?"

One dark brow rose on her forehead when she met my eyes. "Yes, I imagine he will."

"Well, good, 'cause he looks like a right nice young feller to me."

Just then, a teacher walked up to Miss Germane and whispered something into her ear. The rookie chose that moment to take a step closer to me and stick out his right hand. "Name's John," he told me, eyes shining like new blue marbles. "John Jacob Donnelly. But mostly, folks just call me Jake for short."

I was a good six inches taller and had at least thirty pounds on him, yet I couldn't help but admire the strength of his handshake. But I couldn't let him see that, not yet, anyway. So I pumped his arm up and down and said in my deepest voice, "Homer O'Tuathail." For good measure, I added, "I'm twelve years old" like it mattered, because at a place like Dexter, things like age and size mattered a lot.

He leaned closer. "Miss Germane, there," he said under his breath, "she tol' me even afore both my feet was off the bus, that I'm to have a one-on-one with the head master, first thing." He glanced right

48

and left, then narrowed his eyes. "Did you have a one-on-one with him the day you got here?"

"I did." I was only four when my Uncle Joe brought me to Dexter, but I'd never forget a minute of that first day.

"Got any pointers?"

Life in the orphanage had taught me many lessons, among them, think on a question before answering it. So no one was more surprised than me when I blurted, "Well, you might try callin' him 'sir', for starters. And if you interrupt him when he's talkin', he gets so red-faced, you'll think his head is gonna explode, so I'd keep quiet when—"

"Mr. Donnelly," Miss Germane said, "will you follow me, please?" She raised the other brow and aimed a hard stare at me. "Mr. O'Tuathail, you may return the broom to the janitor's closet now." I'd always suspected she knew sweeping was just a way for me to get first glance at the rookies.

"Thanks for the advice, Homer," Jake said, slapping the old hat onto his head.

I nodded, uncertain how I felt about him.

Then he poked out his elbow and offered it to Miss Germane, and when she took it, I knew I was going to like him.

*****

Donaldson's Dormitory was all manner of commotion before Miss Germane flung open the door and pierced our eardrums with her high-pitched "Lights out, gentlemen!" Until then, boys hopped from cot to cot like frogs on lilypads, making the bedsprings squeal like the brakes on an old city bus. Whistles and whoops of laughter bounced off the dorm's stone walls and wood-planked floors.

It was especially noisy that Christmas Eve, because we knew every priest and pastor in Jersey City had 'sermoned' until their parishioners knew the difference between our lives and their own. We pretended not to mind that they saw us as riff-raff; if that's what it took to get them to dig deep, blow the lint off a coin or two, so be it. Because that's what made trucks and rubber balls appear for the boys, baby dolls and stuffed animals for the girls appear under the tree down in the parlor. And if we were real lucky, maybe even some gravy for the dry turkey they'd serve at dinner time.

That night, I couldn't help noticing that the rookie didn't get involved in the rough-housing. He just sat there, cross-legged in the middle of his cot, holding a battered shoebox in his lap. Just being careful, I figured, since it was his first day and all.

So feeling a little sorry for him, I walked over, leaned both forearms on the cold steel footboard of his cot. "What you got there, Jake for Short?"

He aimed those piercing blue eyes at me and stared hard, harder than I'd ever stared at the arithmetic problems Miss Germane scribbled on the board. I couldn't decide if Jake was trying to figure out if I could be trusted, or if my question roused a sad memory. Too many of those at Dexter, and sure I didn't want to be responsible for waking one,

50

especially on Christmas Eve. "It ain't alive, is it?" I teased, grinning as I pointed at the box. "'Cause if it is, Miss Germane will beat your butt for sure."

A little smile lifted one corner of his mouth. "Y'all oughtn't say cuss words, Homer. Cussin' is a sin, y'know."

"Butt isn't a cuss word. Besides...y'all?'" I echoed. "Where you from?"

"Miss'sippi."

"How'd you get all the way from there to here?"

"Well, when my maw died, there weren't no other blood kin to take me in, so I was sent to live with her sister, here in Jersey. And when Aunt Cassie passed...." Jake shrugged. "An' to answer your other question—iffin the thing in this here box was alive—well, if there was, there'd be holes in the top, so's it could breathe, now wouldn't there?"

He'd made a good point, but I wasn't about to admit it. "So if it ain't alive, what is it?"

Jake inhaled, said on the exhale, "This here's...it's...it's a angel."

He said it with the awe and respect folks said God and Jesus. "A...an angel?"

"You one of them young'uns who's got trouble with his ears, Homer?"

Ignoring the insult, I lobbed one of my own. "You ain't of those sissy boys, are ya?"

"If keepin' a Christmas angel in a box makes a feller a sissy boy," he hissed through clenched teeth, "then I reckon I must be a sissy boy."

Well, when he put it that way, it didn't make any sense to me, either. "So what you gonna do with a Christmas angel in a crummy place like this?"

Jake looked at the bouncing boys and the gray walls and the bare wood floor. "I seen worse places."

Worse than Dexter, where it was so noisy a boy couldn't fall asleep unless he was dog-tired? Where it was so crowded, a guy thanked God if he got a minute to shower in private? If there was a worse place, I sure didn't want to see it!

"This is 'zactly the place for an angel," Jake said, "'specially a Christmas angel." He removed the boxtop. "It first belonged to my granmaw, became my maw's when Gran passed on." He sucked in such a big breath that it lifted his shoulders and chin at the same time. "And when my maw passed," he continued, "well, that's how it become mine." He brightened slightly when he added, "Didja notice? Her face is made of porcelain."

He said 'porcelain' like it was something fine, so I nodded, like I knew something about the stuff. Everything about Jake's angel was shiny, from its thick canary-yellow hair to the pale blue shoes poking from under her puffy white dress. The halo on her head and wings on her back, I could tell, had once been the color of the ring Miss Germane's wore. Whether the angel's gold had worn or faded, I couldn't say, but I knew this: She was the prettiest thing I'd ever laid eyes on.

"I saw one of those once," I said, "'bout four years ago, when some church people picked us up in a bus. They took us to see the Nativity play, and there was a big tree beside the stage. It had an angel on top of it."

I stared at its face. Some artist, I supposed, had painted on a tiny, barely-smiling red mouth, black-lashed blue eyes, comma-shaped eyebrows, and pink blushing cheeks. I wondered if her hair felt as soft as it looked. "That angel I saw in town," I began, touching the yellow curls, "wasn't half as pretty as yours."

"We need to get us a Christmas tree."

He said it so matter-of-factly that I laughed out loud, and that brought the others over. "He wants us to get a Christmas tree," I explained as they gathered round, "so he can put his angel on top of it."

In place of the teasing I'd expected, the boys pressed closer still. "A Christmas angel?" said one. "Lemme see it," said another.

Jake tilted the box. "'Twas my grandmaw's," he repeated. "When she passed, it became my own maw's."

"And now that your maw is dead," Tommy asked, mimicking Jake's drawl, "the angel is yours."

"Yep," he said. Then, "So what-say we get busy, gettin' us a Christmas tree!"

"B-b-but how?" Stuttering William demanded. "Any m-m-minute now, it'll be l-l-ights out, and—"

Wiggling his eyebrows, Jake winked. "Get back to makin' noise," he instructed, smirking. "If Miss Germane comes in here and we're all behavin' like li'l angels ourselves, she'll know there's a fox in the hen house, an' we'll never get away with it."

"'A fox in the hen house?'" I echoed. "What in the—"

Jake waved us nearer. "After lights out, me'n Homer, here, will climb out the winder and cut us down a tree."

Tommy crossed both arms over his chest. "How you gonna do that?"

"Y-y-yeah," Stuttering William put in. "W-we ain't got no—"

Jake lifted the white paper surrounding his angel...and exposed a pearl-handled pocket knife. He slid the knife into his trousers' pocket, gave it a light pat-pat-pat. "This here blade ain't goin' to cut down no giant redwood, but then, there ain't room at Dexter for a tree that size, anyway." He pointed. "All's we need is a tree 'bout the size of him."

All eyes went to Tommy, who stood no more than three feet tall. "Ain't gonna be much of a tree," he said, grinning, "if it ain't no bigger than me."

As Jake put the shoebox into his bureau drawer, he said, "Ever seen them fancy ladies in town?"

Giggling and shoving, the boys nodded.

"Well, a Christmas tree is kind like them. It's the doo-dads what make the difference."

If a mirror had been handy just then, I would have bet that my face was as wide-eyed and slack-jawed as everybody else's. Still, as the oldest boy in Donaldson's Dorm I believed I had an obligation to see to it we all kept our feet on the ground. "Doo-dads?" I echoed. "Where we gonna get doo-dads when we don't even know what they are."

Jake's brow crinkled, as if he couldn't believe how dense the lot of us were. Then he looked me in the eye: "Whilst you an' me is out makin' like lumberjacks, these here boys'll come up with somethin' to trim the tree with," he said. "Jus' wait an' see." Then he shoved his bed against the wall, and like a zoo monkey, leaped from headboard to window ledge. "Get back to makin' a racket," he said, "or Miss Germane's gonna come on in here to find out what all the quiet is about!"

Sure enough, when we returned at midnight with a squat, scraggly tree, the boys presented a collection of bent spoons and two-tined forks, the handle from a broken mug, and an assortment of string and twine. When they'd finished hanging the stuff on the tree, Jake handed me his angel. "You're the tallest, Homer. Put 'er up top!"

ONE YEAR LATER:

"What you got there?" Jake asked.

I shoved the blue-lined tablet under my pillow. "Nothin'," I said, feeling the heat of a blush on my cheeks.

"Looked like some kind of school book. You doin' homework?"

"Nah."

Jake opened the drawer where he kept his angel. "Writin' another story?"

I couldn't very well admit it, not with Stuttering William and Tommy standing within earshot. Writing was for girls. And girlie-boys.

His hand shot out and pulled the tablet from under my pillow.

"Hey, give it back!" I hollered, grabbing for it.

But quick as an eyeblink, Jake took off down the hall and locked himself into the janitor's closet. He knew as well as I did that if I kicked up too big a fuss, every boy in Donaldson's Dorm would want to know why. I had no choice but to sit quietly...and plan the way I'd tear him apart once he opened that door.

Nearly an hour passed before he called through the keyhole. "Homer?"

"What."

"These stories of yours.... Wow."

Did that mean he liked them? I licked my lips. "Gimme my tablet back," I snarled.

"Y'all are special, Homer. You know that, right?"

They called Fat Freddie "special"; grown-up talk for not too bright. I felt my hands ball into fists. Oh, he was going to get it good when he came out of there, for sure!

"Iffin y'wanna clobber me for swipin' your book, go right ahead. Readin' your stories was worth a good beatin'." Slowly, he opened the door and handed me the tablet. Head down and hands pocketed, he walked slowly back to the dorm.

"Hey. Where do you think you're going?"

"To get my angel."

56

I caught up with him. "But...but it ain't even close to Christmas."

He stopped so fast, I nearly crashed into him.

"Save that surprised look for somebody else. I know you seen me talkin' to her when I need to puzzle out a problem."

Kids did all sorts of goofy things to get by at Dexter. Talking to Christmas tree angels didn't seem all that strange, compared to some of the stuff I'd seen. "What're you gonna ask her?"

"You'll see," he said. Back in the dorm, he sat on the edge of his cot and held the angel in his hands. "So what do you think?" he asked her. "Is it 'sissy' for a boy to be writin' stories down in a notebook?" He held her small face to his ear and, nodding, he smiled.

No one else was listening. What could it hurt to play along? I moved closer. "So...?"

Gently, he tucked her back into the shoebox, put the box back into his drawer. "She said there ain't nothin' girlie 'bout a boy tellin' stories that make other people feel good. She says that's just what Jesus did, an' nobody ever called him a sissy."

I sat on my own cot, swallowing and staring, until Jake got up. He was almost in the hallway when he turned and said, "I'll just bet if you sent those stories to a magazine, they'd pay you for 'em."

Two years later, when I was fourteen and Jake was twelve, I packed my cardboard suitcase with those stories Jake read that day—and dozens more I'd written since—and prepared to leave Dexter. He walked with me to the big iron gates. "You'll do fine out there, Homer."

"Did your angel tell you that?"

Smiling, Jake said, "You always seem to know what's important, and that'll stand you in good stead, no matter where you go or what you do."

"That's good to hear," I said, meaning it.

"Promise me something?"

"If I can."

"Don't quit writin' them stories of yours. One day, they're gonna make you rich and famous."

I laughed. "Yeah, and you're gonna be a comedian."

"One more promise?"

This time I didn't hesitate. "Sure." I liked the kid. Fact was, Jake was the closest thing to a brother I'd ever had.

"If anything happens to me, will you take care of my angel? She means a lot, bein' she's all I have to remember my maw by, so...."

The idea of a world without Jake, well, it wasn't a place I cared to live. "That's just crazy talk. You're gonna live forev—"

"We hafta stay in touch, and not like them others who leave here sayin' they's gonna." Winking, he socked my shoulder. "It'll be like we're brothers."

"Sure," I repeated.

And then I left Dexter for good.

I hitched a ride from Jersey to New York City, and got a job as a short order cook in a diner near the theater district. Every night, alone in my room above the kitchen, I scribbled on blue-lined tablets....

I saw Jake just twice after that, but every now and then, when I got a yearning for that feet-on-the-ground, Jake Donnelly brand of common sense, I'd pick up a phone, knowing even before hearing his slow southern drawl that I'd feel better about my life, about myself, when we said goodbye. Because Jake meant to make a difference in people's lives. In his presence, fat girls felt thin, ugly girls felt pretty; dumb boys felt smart, and scared boys felt brave. And boys who didn't believe they had the talent or the courage to show their stories to publishers, tried.

I was still fourteen when I got up the nerve to mail one of my stories to a magazine. By nineteen, I'd been published dozens of times. And since then, I've enjoyed material success like most men only dream about.

Couple of years back, I got an invitation to Christmas at the White House. There were trees everywhere, but not one could compare to my first one at Dexter Domicile for Displace Juveniles.

I owe you a big one, Jake, and that's never more clear to me than at Christmastime.

The End

FIVE YEARS LATER:

"Homer, schweetheart," Bobby said, "so what's up with your answering machine? I've been trying to get hold of you for days."

"Don't have one up here. Don't want one. Don't need one."

"Letterman's people have been hounding me all week. They want you, baby, want you bad."

"Once upon a time, I would have jumped at an invitation to hawk a book-turned-movie on Dave's show. But things are different now. I'm different now."

"Well, that's true." Bobby snickered. "Remember the time you stood Letterman up? Lucky for you he doesn't hold a grudge."

Homer had gained his fame with gritty detective novels, but the story of Jake's angel had come straight from his heart, and touched a national nerve.

"Homer. Baby. We're talking big bucks here."

"Y'know, not so long ago, a statement like that would have dilated my pupils. Now, it means next to nothing." If big bucks hadn't been the center of his world, maybe he'd have a rich life, a loving wife, couple of kids and grandkids.... "I like the way I live," he lied. "Things are simple, uncomplicated."

"But Homer, the publicity...."

He'd said the same thing five years ago, when Tri-Adon made the offer to turn Jake's Angel into a major motion picture. Homer had agreed to sign, on one condition:

Profits from the book and the movie would create a national organization to provide loving homes for parentless kids. Nobody, not even Homer, had expected Jake's Angel to set box office records, earning enough to build a Paradise House in dozens of cities, each staffed by child-care specialists known as "Jake's Angels".

Jake would have loved the irony.

"About Letterman…."

Homer laughed quietly. "Sure. Why not. Dave can write a check to Paradise House instead of Homer O'Tuathail...on the air. Talk about publicity!"

Bobby sighed. "So what are you working on?"

"Down, boy," Homer said. "You'll have the manuscript before it's due on my editor's desk."

"I wasn't worried."

"Liar."

Chuckling, Bobby said, "What do you do up there in that tiny cabin all by yourself?"

West Virginia's Yew Mountains provided some of the most satisfying vistas Homer had ever seen, and thanks to his success, he'd seen most of the world. "This and that," he said, knowing full well that if he admitted how much he enjoyed stacking wood, tending his vegetables, writing stories, Bobby wouldn't believe him anyway.

"Mind if I ask you a serious question?" Bobby asked.

Homer chuckled. "Long as you don't mind hearing it's none of your business."

"What's with you lately? I mean, seriously. You used to love livin' in the fast lane, seeing your face on supermarket tabloids, throwing wild parties, pretty girl on each arm. You were the envy of every red-blooded American male."

It had taken a lifetime, but Homer had finally found his place in the world. Looking up at the Buster Brown shoebox on the shelf above his desk, he smiled. Material things? Parties? Women? These past two years, he'd lived well, better than ever, without them. He took a deep breath of clean mountain air, let it out slowly.

"Let's just say...I'm keeping a promise to Jake."

Sly's Christmas Surprise

By Brenda K. Hendricks

"Samuel Lee Yeager, let's go! The deal of the hour awaits." Mom's voice ascended the stairs, bounced off the hallway walls, and penetrated my bedroom door like the cry of the Alamo.

My friends had called me Sly since first grade, but Mom called me Samuel...never Sam or Sammy...always Samuel. And when she got impatient, she used my full name.

"I'm on my way." I rooted through the stack of books and homework cluttering my dresser top, found a rubber band, and twisted it around the end of my thick, dark-brown braid. Flinging it over my shoulder, I rushed down the hall. My braid tapped the middle of my back as I skipped steps to meet my mom at the front door. I brushed a strand of her smoke-colored curls away, and leaning down, kissed her forehead.

"Good morning," I said with as much of a smile as my sleepy face could muster. I opened the door for her. A gust of early December wind froze my smile in place. The car's engine revved as Dad jumped out and ran around to open the passenger's door for Mom. Like I couldn't have done that. I slid onto the seat behind hers, thankful Dad had warmed up the Lincoln.

Most seventeen-year-old boys had the option of sleeping in on the day after Thanksgiving, but not me. The Pastor Brandon Yeager, his wife Dottie, and their two sons had a tradition to uphold. Christmas would not arrive unless we got out there at five in the morning to meet and greet our neighbors in the wild, Black-Friday-bargain blitz. My brother, BJ, aged out this year. He left for college the middle of August, and since he was now three states west of Pennsylvania, my parents excused him. He said he was sorry he was going to miss the shopping extravaganza. He almost sounded sincere.

Personally, I lost my zeal for the holiday about a decade ago when I realized the big guy in the red suit had faked out little kids for centuries and had gotten away with it. Since then, the entire gift giving/getting scene made no sense to me. Mom and Dad fussed, debated, compared, complained, and pondered until they finally picked out useless items no one would ever buy for themselves for any reason...seriously. In return, we received gifts that left us scratching our heads and wondering what were they thinking?

I, on the other hand, had a simple solution for the whole getting/giving frenzy. Invite everyone to whom we wanted to give Christmas presents to our house and form a huge circle. Dad would whip a fifty out of his wallet and hand it to the person on his right. That person would hand it to the next person and so on until the fifty bucks made its way back to Dad. He'd stuff it back into his wallet. We'd all sing Joy to the World and thank God we didn't have to make any returns the next day. The best part would be sleeping late on Black Friday and leaving the gnashing and biting to the bargain-hunting beasts. And the next day, I could con Dad out of the fifty bucks....

I didn't hate the holiday or the idea of a gift exchange. I just thought there had to be an easier approach...one that offered little less hassle and lots more "zzz's."

Leaning my head back, I shut my eyes and processed the results of my current science project.

*****

Monday morning I awoke at 10:15 a.m. Most schools in Central Pa closed Monday and Tuesday after Thanksgiving, which was way cool as far as I was concerned. Christmas carols greeted me as I tiptoed down the backstairs into the kitchen. I gulped down two cream-filled doughnuts and chugged about a quart of milk from the container before replacing it in the fridge. Grabbing my jacket from the back of a chair, I shrugged it on and checked the pockets. Mom's car keys were still there. My escape was almost a done deal as I reached for the doorknob....

"Samuel." Mom's cream-filled tone only meant one thing—she had errands for me to run. "You weren't leaving without saying goodbye, were you?"

"Who me?" I turned and meandered through the maze of already-wrapped Christmas boxes and bags that led to the living room. "Would I do that?"

"Of course not." Mom sat in the middle of the floor, waist-deep in wrapping paper, ribbons, and bows, resembling a kid on Christmas morning only in reverse mode. She had presents for every member of every disadvantaged family in the neighborhood, whether they attended the Dutton Community Worship Center or not. The gift-wrapping scene was definitely her favorite part of the season. She smiled up at me. "I need you to deliver some of these packages today."

"Aw, Mom. I had plans to shoot some hoops with Jaden and the rest of my buddies at the gym this morning."

"Good! The gifts in the kitchen go to people from High Street to Mill Street. It's on your way."

"Can't I do it after the game?"

"You know the rules, son. Chores first. Games later. Remember? You agreed to make these deliveries a week ago."

"But the game will be over before I get them delivered."

"Why not call your buddies and tell them you'll be late. I'm sure they'll wait for you."

"Yeah, right. Like that's gonna happen." I returned to the kitchen. "Which ones?"

"All of them."

"All of them?" I looked back at the stacks of boxes full of gifts I had just walked around. Mom did Christmas in a big way...not just one small gift for each home. Oh no! Several gifts for everyone in the household. We were talking huge. "The game'll be over before I get them all in the car."

"Some of the boxes go to the same house." Mom walked into the kitchen, dusting off her jeans. "It's only ten houses in all for today. We can help soften the economy's ill effects on our neighbors by giving them these simple gifts. It's that worth your sacrifice." She loaded my arms with gift bags and boxes, opened the door, and grabbing another box, accompanied me to the car. "I've called everyone to let them know you're coming. If we keep them in order, it shouldn't be too difficult for you to deliver everything in a fairly decent amount of time just like BJ did for three years. You don't have to visit with anyone. Just take the gifts inside then leave."

I suddenly missed my brother more than ever. Mom and I made several more trips to the car, stuffing the backseat and trunk full. At least, she had it all organized. After she went back in the house, I slid behind the steering wheel and shot a text to Jaden. He was probably already at the gym and wouldn't hear the phone…figures.

Mrs. Shaffer was the first on the list. The white-haired, pudgy woman answered the door with a wide grin that lifted her wrinkles. Grabbing my arm, she pulled me inside. She stuck the box of gifts under the smallest artificial tree I've ever seen and ushered me into her kitchen against my will for cookies and milk. "A growing boy needs sustenance," she said. Far be it from me to argue with a senior citizen and refuse homemade chocolate chip cookies. The milk turned out to be hot chocolate with marshmallows. I lost a half-hour there. She made me promise to come back before Christmas…a promise I intended to keep. Her cookies were the best.

On the way to the next stop, I checked my text messages. Jaden hadn't responded. I didn't bother sending another one. The house, two blocks from Mrs. Shaffer's, needed paint. The steps creaked as I approached the front door, sat the first box on the porch, and backtracked to the car. Managing to step on the same loose boards when I returned with the other three boxes, I spied a girl, maybe twelve, peeking through a curtain at a side window.

"It's okay," I said. "I'm Sam, Pastor Yeager's son. We have Christmas presents for you and the rest of your family." The boxes in my arms grew heavier by the second. I was tempted to set them on the porch and leave, but before I made up my mind, the door opened slowly.

"Come in," the girl said. Straggly brown hair spiked out from underneath her pink baseball cap. Despite the cap's brim, I caught a twinkle in her brown eyes. "Put the boxes over there on the coffee table."

I followed her direction and set the boxes on the table. The aroma of fresh baked bread made my mouth water even though I was full from Mrs. Shaffer's cookies. I felt awkward, like I should say or do something. I extended my hand as though I were a church greeter. "I'm Samuel Yeager."

The girl giggled. "You said that. I'm Evie." Her smile brightened her pale face. "I'll be right back." She disappeared into another room and quickly returned with an oblong package. "Mom said to give you this. She had to run some errands."

I took the gift…still warm. A loaf of bread was my guess. My mouth watered again. "Thanks."

"Evie!" A boy a head shorter than Evie skidded into the room in his stocking feet. Dragging a scruffy blanket, a smaller boy toddled behind him. "Jacob needs a tissue, and I need some juice," the older boy said then slid back into the other room.

"I'll get you both a drink in a minute, Mattie." Evie pulled a tissue out of her pocket and wiped the little guy's nose. He squirmed and squawked, knocking Evie's hat to the floor. The crown of her head was totally bald. I stifled a gasp. But I couldn't stop the shock from firing up my face. Her hand immediately stroked her hairless scalp reddened with embarrassment as she picked up her hat and replaced it.

"I'm not sick," she said, facing me with a thin smile. I returned one. "I have a disease called alopecia totalis." She scrunched her lips together and swallowed hard, obviously determined not to cry. "I'll be totally bald by Christmas. Some present, huh?"

"Can't you get a wig?" I ran my hand down the back of my head.

"Don't worry. It's not contagious, honest. Wigs are expensive."

"There are organizations like—"

"Yeah, we're on a waiting list which could take who knows how long…years maybe."

Jacob sneezed. Evie wiped his nose again and picked him up. "I better get him some juice and try to get him to take a nap before Mom gets home. Thanks for the gifts. Hope you enjoy the bread. I made it myself."

"Thanks, Evie. I'm sure we will." I walked out with a ton of ideas brewing in my head. I wasn't sure why I had to help her, but I knew I had to. I rushed to my car and, ignoring the rest of the boxes in the backseat, drove straight to the school. I parked next to Jaden's car and sprinted to the gym.

Several guys formed a huddle in the middle of the court. The game was obviously over already. I ran over to Jaden and Rusty who sat on the floor with their backs against the wall, wiping their sweaty brows.

We had been friends since pre-school. They went to our church. Jaden lived next door to me, and Rusty lived next to him. We played super heroes and called ourselves The Protectors in first grade, became "blood brothers" in fifth grade, and redefined our role as The Protectors in seventh. In eighth grade, a few other guys joined us. We all vowed to defend weaker students from bullies and never to cut our hair as a symbol of our private club.

"Nice of you to finally show up." Rusty's scowl told me they had lost. His red mane pulled back into a ponytail frizzed in all directions.

"I texted," I said in self-defense. "How bad was it?"

"Bad enough." Jaden stood. Although he had to stretch to meet my six-foot-three frame, he was a good basketball player. He flung his ink-black hair over his shoulder and socked his fists on his hips. "What happened to you? We really needed you out there."

"Mom made me deliver Christmas presents."

"Figures," Rusty said as he rose to his full six-and- a-half feet. "I'm going to get a shower." He and Jaden turned and walked toward the locker room.

"No, wait!" I darted after them. "I have something really urgent to talk to you guys about."

They stopped and looked me square in the eye. They were none too happy with me. I knew I had to make this crazy idea stick.

"I met a girl, Evie. She's about twelve."

"She's way too young for you, Sly," Rusty smirked.

"Duh!" I said. "She has a disease called alopecia totalis."

"Sounds nasty." Jaden grimaced.

"It is," I continued. "She'll be totally bald by Christmas."

"Is she in a lot of pain?" Jaden's eyes showed his inability to deal with even the thought of suffering.

"No," I said.

"Then buy her a wig," Rusty said. He started to walk in the other direction, but I grabbed his arm.

"It's not that simple. Wigs are expensive and the waiting lists are long," I said. "I have a plan, but I'm gonna need you guys to help me pull it off and maybe the rest of the gang."

Rusty sighed. "Okay. Let's hear it."

"Jaden, remember the funny stories your grandpa used to tell about how he and your grandmother met?" I asked.

He gave me a quizzical look. "The ones about Grandma teaching wig making classes?"

"Yeah, is there any truth to it?"

"Yeah. They even volunteered several times to help make wigs to give to children like the girl you're talking about. I remember watching them…fascinating process."

74

"So your grandpa hasn't lost the skill."

"No...oh, I getcha. You want Grandpa to make a wig for Evie."

"Yep. Do you think he'd have time to get it done for Christmas?"

"I have no clue—"

"Where are you gonna get the hair?" Rusty interrupted. I just glared at him. "Oh wait," he said, "you want us to donate our hair."

"Bingo!" I grinned.

Someone behind me flicked my braid. I didn't have to turn to know it was Grady Trout, one of the school bullies. Out of the corner of my eye, I saw Trout strut across the gym. Several of his friends followed him to the water cooler where a group of underclassmen was hanging out.

I tilted my head in that direction. Jaden's and Rusty's eyes shifted to the trouble spot then back to me. They nodded. Mike and Wayne, two other members of The Protectors, joined us as we marched across the room.

I grasped Trout's shoulder just as he picked up one of the little guys by the back of his shirt. "I know you weren't going to dunk Tony in the water fountain again today," I said.

"You gonna stop me, PK?" Trout's brain was the size of a pea. He thought PK stood for ponytail kreep...he even spelled it out several times. We laughed so hard we couldn't tell him creep was spelled with a c not a k. What a bonehead.

"I already have," I said holding a straight face and tightening my grip. My buds and I had created enough of a diversion simply by walking toward them for the rest of the kids to hightail it out of there. Poor Tony, still dangling and squirming in Trout's grip, looked at me as though I was dressed in red and blue spandex and could climb walls while spewing spider webs out of my wrists to bind the villain.

"Put the kid down now, Trout," Rusty said, "and we'll all walk away as though you weren't the ugliest dork in our school."

I really wished he hadn't said that.

Trout dropped Tony, who scooted out of the gym faster than a scared cat. The bully swung a fist at me. I ducked. Unfortunately, Mike caught the punch in the nose. Blood squirted out everywhere, but it didn't stop Mike. He decked one of the bullies. The fight was on. I smacked Trout up alongside the head and then caught one of his fists in the eye. I heard thuds and groans coming from the others as Trout and I duked it out. Although we both staggered from exhaustion, neither of us backed off.

Trout right-hooked me in the jaw. I shook my head to ward off the pain. Was that a siren I heard? Trout lowered his fists. We glared at one another then scanned the gym. Everyone was gone. The siren grew louder. Trout's eyes met mine. I wondered if fear creased on my face like it had his.

This wasn't the first time we'd fought on school property. Trout and his buddies tormented the little kids all the time. The Protectors defended them. But there had always been a teacher around the corner to stop us before we beat the snot out of one another. Today, however, the coach must've left early or something. At least, I hadn't seen an adult since I'd been here.

The siren ceased, but the red lights from the cop car flashed through the windows. It had definitely stopped close by.

Trout looked kind of green around the edges like he was going to puke or something. We both knew our goose was cooked, and there was nowhere to run.

The door swung open. Officer Steeple, a local cop, stepped inside. Man, he was big. His shoulders filled the doorframe. I wasn't sure, but I could've sworn he had to duck to enter. The scowl on his face made him look like a pit-bull ready to attack. He always looked so pleasant in church. What a difference a uniform makes.

"Oh crud," Trout said under his breath.

"Yeah." I seconded the statement. It was the first and probably the last thing we'd ever agree on. My eye throbbed. My knuckles ached. But I knew the beating I took here was nothing compared to the verbal beating I'd get when I got home.

Officer Steeple walked over to us and stopped directly in front of Trout. I heard him gulp.

"It looks like a massacre happened here. Anyone else involved in this little brawl besides the two of you?"

"No, sir," Trout said without missing a beat. The officer looked at me. I shrugged. He turned back to Trout.

"What's your name, boy?" Steeple pulled a pen and small notebook out of his pocket.

"Grady Trout."

"Where do you live, Grady?"

"112 East Pennsdale Lane."

The address sounded vaguely familiar to me. But I was too worn out to give it any more thought.

Steeple jotted it down. "Your mom or dad there now?"

"I don't know. Maybe."

"You know where one of them can be reached?"

"I have their cell numbers."

"Good. You call them and tell them I'll be paying them a visit shortly. Go home and stay put until I get there. Understood?"

"Yes, sir." Trout ran toward the door.

"Grady," the officer called over his shoulder. Trout stopped dead in his tracks but didn't turn to face Steeple. "Don't try to hide out somewhere because I will find you."

Trout nodded and ran out the door.

I took two steps toward the exit.

"Whoa. No one said you could leave," Office Steeple said, pressing his hand against my chest. "Samuel Yeager, what will the pastor say? Think about how this is going make him look. Your brother never got into any trouble like this. Come on, I'll take you home."

Everything always boiled down to how it made my dad look. Never mind that I could barely see out of my left eye…how did that make me look? And, of course, BJ never got into any trouble. He was the perfect son. Never mind that I got this shiner and fat lip defending a little runt that couldn't stand up for himself. Nope…no matter what I did, I was the black sheep of the family, as my mother had put it more than once.

"I'll be all right. I have Mom's car…." I slapped my forehead. "I have Christmas presents to deliver."

"Not looking like that you don't. You'd totally humiliate your parents if you showed up at anyone's house all bloodied up like that."

I glanced at my shirt. Steeple was right. I couldn't show my face or my shirt around town. I couldn't go home looking like this either or without delivering those boxes. My parents would take turns screaming at me. I'll probably be grounded for life. Good thing we don't believe in reincarnation or I'd be grounded for my next two lives. Like Trout had said, "Oh crud."

*****

At the house, I opened the door and motioned for Officer Steeple to enter first. I stepped in and closed the door, standing directly behind him.

"Officer Steeple, what are you doing here?" Mom gasped. "Something's happened. Where's Samuel?" Her voice cracked.

The officer took a side step, exposing me…and my shiner. Mom's hand cupped her mouth as she jumped to her feet. "Oh, dear heavens! What on earth did you do? Did you wreck my car? Have you been checked out by a paramedic? Should I call 911?" She always hit the panic button and asked logical questions later.

Steeple made his way through the wrapping paraphernalia and grasped Mom's elbow, guiding her to the couch. "Maybe you should sit down. Is Pastor Brandon home?"

"He's in the study." Mom sat and yelled over her shoulder. "Brandon, you need to come out here right away."

Dad stretched as he walked down the hall. I wanted to hide behind Steeple again when I caught the look on Dad's face. It morphed from quizzical to concern to disgust. No panic button there. He knew what had happened without being told.

Steeple met Dad at the end of the hall and, like a butler, escorted him to the couch. Dad refused to sit.

"There was a fight at the school gym," the officer said. "Samuel and another boy were beating one another's brains out when I got the call from another kid and arrived on the scene. I figured I'd make sure Samuel got home safe. He'll do the explaining. I've got to get to the other boy's house before he decides to hide out somewhere."

The officer shook my parents' hands, said his goodbyes, and walked across the room. I opened the door for him. He paused. "Meet back at the gym in about an hour. You and Mr. Trout can spend the rest of the afternoon scrubbing up the mess you made. Who knows…it may help you resolve your differences."

"Yes, sir," I said as I shut the door. Turning to face my parents, I lightly touched my swollen eye. Nothing could help resolve the differences between Trout and me.

Mom jumped up, rushed to the kitchen, and returned with two bags of frozen vegetables—one for my eye and the other for my jaw.

"Sit, son," Dad finally said as he eased onto the couch. I found my way to the recliner and sat on the edge, propping my elbows on my knees and leaning into the bags of veggies in my hands. "I'd like an explanation."

"You must've delivered those packages in record time." Mom returned to her seat beside Dad. They both glared at me.

"I didn't exactly get them all delivered."

"What?" they said simultaneously. Then it started, both of them talking at once. Wah wah wah. Did they know they sounded like a pair of geese arguing about which way was south? I tried to listen but couldn't understand a word either of them said.

"Don't you have anything to say for yourself?" Dad's voice finally prevailed. "What were you doing at the gym?"

"Well, I—"

They started again. If they'd let me explain, they might be proud of me just once.

"It was about your hair again, wasn't it?" Dad's voice rose to the top again. "It's about time you get that mane cut and look proper. You'll soon be checking out colleges, and you sure won't make a good impression with that hair."

He always turned every conversation into an argument about my hair. I stood and tossed the frozen veggies on the recliner.

"The fight had nothing to do with my hair. And if a college judges people by the length of their hair, I don't want to go there. If you'd just let me explain—"

"Explain what? That you're rebellious and selfish, always thinking about what works for you without giving any thought to how your actions affect other members of this family? I'm the—"

"Pastor of the largest church in our area. Yeah, I'm well aware of that. And I'm the pastor's son, and I'm expected to behave like an angel just like BJ. Well, I'm not BJ. I get things wrong for the right reasons. You just never take the time to find out what those reasons are."

"Wrong is wrong, Samuel," Dad countered. "All the reasoning in the world can't turn wrong into right. You're grounded for the next two weeks, which means no car, no gym, no social activities, no—"

"I'm well aware of the connotations." I handed over my phone and stomped to the door, slamming it hard on the way out.

"Where do you think you're going?" Dad's voice echoed through the neighborhood. Apparently, screaming at your kid for all the world to hear was acceptable.

"I have to meet Officer Steeple at the gym, remember?"

"I'll drive you."

"I'll walk."

I zipped up my jacket, pulling the collar up around my ears, then I tucked my hands in my pockets. The wind whipped snowflakes around my head. I took the long way through the park and paused for a break at the pond. A thin layer of ice crusted the water's edge. Several ducks fluttered their wings. Why hadn't they flown south like normal waterfowl? What I wouldn't give for wings to fly south about now.

*****

After we finished the dishes that evening, Dad dismissed me to go to my room with a reminder that that's where I'd be spending all my free time for the next two weeks, as though I had somehow forgotten.

I trudged upstairs and sank into the chair at my desk. At least, they hadn't confiscated my computer. I logged into Facebook and spilled my guts in a private message to my closest ex-friends.

feeling like the world's biggest loser right now. trying to help that little kid at the gym today got me grounded for two weeks. trout shows up to help scrub the gym, officer steeple's orders, and laughs about his dad patting him on the back for beating up the pk. oh and thanks a lot for deserting me. you're all a bunch of morons.

Too ticked to stay on and wait for their replies, I flipped through some games but didn't feel much like playing any of them. Besides, one of The Protectors would most definitely be on and start a chat about how it wasn't their fault they all got out before Steeple arrived. I'd had enough confrontation for one day.

Pulling my microscope to the front of the desk, I opened my science notes on the computer. I scooted my chair over to the mini fridge Dad had bought me to store petri dishes of fungi, bacteria, and other stuff Mom wouldn't allow in the kitchen fridge. I grabbed a vial of bacteria then wheeled my chair back to the desk, slipped on a pair of latex gloves, and got to work. Nothing released my frustration quite like exploring the invisible-to-the-naked-eye world.

As I watched those tiny organisms swim, I imagined myself reduced to their size, entering their world, and living their life. It brought me close to understanding what Christmas was really about....

The immenseness of God reduced, yet intact, and contained in the shell of a baby. No wonder angels announced his arrival to the only ones awake and semi-willing to listen. It would've been like me yelling at the amoeba squirming on my slide, "Hey, I'm going to shrink myself, jump into your world, and make things better for you." Why would I do that? Why did God? That was what I had to figure out.

Lost in my thoughts, I studied slide after slide until my eyes blurred. I typed up some notes, replaced all my paraphernalia, and stretched out across the bed. While pondering my becoming a single-celled organism to God becoming man, I drifted off.

Clink. Clink.

I opened my eyes and looked at the alarm clock—11:32 p.m.

Clink. Clink.

I blinked to focus.

Clink. Clink.

The noise was coming from the window. I walked across the room and peeked out. Jaden and Rusty stood below, waving frantically. I should've known. We always waited until our parents were in bed then sneaked out to visit the one that was grounded. Slipping into my shoes, I shrugged on my coat and tiptoed down the back stairs, through the kitchen, and out the door.

The crisp air sent a chill down my neck. A bazillion glistening stars reminded again of the vastness of God and a baby in a manager.

"Sorry for cutting out on you at the gym," Jaden said. "I yelled at you twice, but you and Trout were so involved, I guess you didn't hear me."

"At least you tried." I slapped his back to let him know I was okay with it now.

"I yelled too," Rusty's voice quivered from the cold.

"Fighting is intense." I socked Rusty's arm. "It's cool."

"I talked to Gramps about the wig." Jaden smiled. "He said it'd be pushing it, but he thought he could manage it by Christmas."

"Tell him it's a no go," I said sheepishly.

"What do you mean a no go?" Rusty grimaced and pulled off his cap to reveal a head full of red curls…short red curls.

Jaden yanked off his hat. His braid was gone too. "Gramps said he'd have to get started immediately. So we all, Mike, Wayne, Clair … all of us let Gramps cut off our braids right away."

"Then he should have enough hair. I'm not cutting mine now."

"You have to. Gramps says he needs at least one more. When we told him how thick yours is, he said that'd probably be just enough."

"I said I'm not going through with it. Dad ended his lecture with, 'get a haircut.' I can't let him win. It's the principle of the thing."

"You're right about one thing, Sly. You are a loser," Rusty said. "If I could squeeze your drop of blood out of my finger, right now, I'd do it." He stomped off.

"You and your stupid principles." Jaden glared at me. "There are higher principles than yours, Sly. Like the principle of helping others. That's what we've agreed The Protectors was about … taking the opportunity to do good. We have an opportunity to do something really great for that little girl. Our hair will grow back. Hers won't." He sighed. "You stick to your principles and I guarantee one thing…it's the end of The Protectors." I caught the glint of anger in his eyes as he turned away from me. He ran across the yard and entered his back door.

I trudged inside and upstairs. In my room, I kicked off my shoes, bouncing one off the wall. I paused. No sound from my parents meant they hadn't heard the thud. I tossed my jacket on the chair, changed into my sweats, and flopped on my bed, my mind racing. The embarrassment in Evie's pleading eyes, the fear in Tony's, the hatred in Trout's, the disappointment in Dad's, and the anger in Jaden's haunted me like the ghouls and monsters in a video game. My head throbbed. I felt smaller and lonelier than a single cell on an observation slide.

I sat on the edge of my bed, rubbing my temples. I paced the floor. I sat at my computer and logged into Facebook. Rusty and Jaden were there. I sent them an invitation for a closed group chat. They both responded immediately, much to my surprise.

Sly: need help

Rusty: duh

Jaden: u getting ur hair cut or not? time's crucial swallow ur pride man

I intuitively swallowed. Pride and principles didn't go down so easily.

Jaden: think of someone else for once

Sly: doesn't my shiner count

Rusty: not so sure every fight uve fought was for anyone but urself and ur principles

Sly: how did gramps do it

Jaden: he tied a rubber band at the top of our braids cut above the band then styled what remained

Rusty: quit being such a moron sly just getter done

Sly: will sleep on it

I signed out and went back to bed. Ghouls with the eyes of the day's confrontations haunted me. I paced. I peeked through my microscope. At the window, I gazed at the stars. I paced again. I pulled my braid over my shoulder and studied its sheen, thickness, and color. Grandma always said, "It's a shame that beautiful head of hair was wasted on a boy." I smiled as I twisted a rubber band around the top of it about an inch from the base of my skull. She would've been pleased with what I was about to do.

*****

The next morning, I rushed down the back stairs into the kitchen. Mom stood facing the stove, flipping pancakes, our usual Tuesday breakfast. Dad sat at the table with his nose buried in the Daily News.

"You're up early for the last day of vacation," Mom said without turning from her skillet.

"I promised to help Jaden's grandpa with a project." I zipped up my coat and yanked my cap over my ears.

"You're grounded. Or did you forget already?" Dad sipped his coffee, but didn't look my way.

"I … I made the promise before I was grounded, Dad." I stretched the truth a bit. But I said it apologetically.

"Did you say Jaden's grandfather?"

"Yes."

"I suppose since it's him, I'll let you go. But don't go anywhere else and be back by lunchtime."

As he peeked over the paper, I darted out the door and called, "Thanks." Goes to show how observant my parents are. Maybe I could wear this hat until my hair grows back, and they'd never notice.

"Samuel!" Dad yelled. I back stepped and opened the door a crack. "Ask Jaden's grandfather to do me a favor and straighten out that hack job you gave yourself."

*****

Christmas Day, I woke early just like I used to when I was a kid—full of anxiety and anticipation. I rushed down the front stairs where the rest of the family waited. I faked a surprised look at all the gifts under the tree and hurried to the kitchen. BJ, Dad, and I sat at our usual place around the table while Mom dished out the usual oatmeal topped with the usual brown sugar, raisins, and walnuts. I gobbled mine down and tried to hurry the rest of the family. But Dad was in his usual Christmas-conversation mode and wouldn't be rushed.

Forty-five minutes later, we made our way back into the living room and sat in our usual circle by the tree. Dad read the Christmas story from Luke then prayed. He read the "to" and "from" names on each gift as he handed them out one by one. I'd never realized how slow and torturous this process was until today.

I ripped the wrappings off, threw them in the garbage bag Mom always provided, and stacked my new belongings on a pile in my usual spot under the tree.

"Thanks, everyone," I said as I stood. "May I be excused now?"

Dad furrowed his brows.

Mom scowled. "What's your rush?"

"Do you ever stop pushing your luck, bro?"

"I have a gift to deliver to a friend."

"Can't it wait 'til later?" Dad stood to face me.

"It's really important to me, Dad."

Mom stood and clasped my hand. "But—"

"Thanks, Dad." I shrugged on my coat. "I'll be back in an hour. I promise."

*****

I ran the five blocks to the Brubakers' residence. I knocked on the door and shivered as I waited for someone to open it. It gave a mournful creak, and I looked up into hateful eyes....

"Trout? What are you doing here?" I stepped back, clutching the box in my hands.

"I live here. What are you doing here?"

"I brought this gift for Evie."

"Stay away from my sister, Sly." Trout's eyes grew more hateful than ever.

"Your sister? But—"

"We have different fathers. You want to make something of it?"

"No."

"That's what I thought. Now make like a snake and slither off my—"

"Grady, is that Samuel Yeager?" A soft voice called and the door opened wider.

"Yeah, Mom. I told him—"

"I heard what you told him." Mrs. Brubaker stood behind Trout and tucked a strand of mousy brown hair behind her ear. "I've been expecting him." She smiled at me. "Come in, Samuel."

Trout stepped aside. I entered the living room. The two younger boys, still in footie pajamas, sat on the floor with their dad playing with their new erector set. Trout stepped over the set and flopped in a chair.

"Nice to meet you, Samuel. I'm Evie's dad, Dave." Mr. Brubaker shook my hand then gestured toward the boys on the floor. "I guess you met Mattie and Jacob a couple of weeks ago when you delivered the presents."

"Yep. Hi guys." I high-fived each of them. They giggled.

"Have a seat, Samuel." Mrs. Brubaker motioned to a chair next to Trout. I sat, still holding tight to Evie's gift. Mrs. Brubaker sat on the sofa facing us. "Evie, you have company."

Evie adjusted her ball cap as she walked into the room. "Hey, Sam."

"Hey, Evie. I brought you something." I stood and handed her the package.

"Me?" A broad grin stretched across her face. "Your family already gave me a beautiful dress and boots."

"Those were from my parents. This is from my friends and me."

She sat on the sofa beside her mother and carefully undid the wrapping paper as though she thought the gift might be a prank. Her mother winked at me and grinned. Mr. B. and the younger boys shifted their attention to Evie and the unexpected gift. Even Trout leaned forward with an intent interest. Evie lifted the lid and pulled out the Styrofoam head form with the auburn wig attached. Her eyes widened. Had it frightened her? Tears streamed down her face. Had I offended her? She wept in her mother's arms, clutching the wig with both hands.

What did I do wrong? I wanted to run out before Trout punched me out for making his sister cry, but my feet froze on the spot.

Evie finally looked up at me. "Thank you so much," she whispered as she wiped the tears from her eyes. "It's the best Christmas present ever."

"Can you wait a few minutes, Samuel?" Mrs. Brubaker asked.

I nodded.

She and Evie disappeared into another room. I sat back in the chair, propped my ankle on my knee, and nervously wiggled my foot. I peeked out the corner of my eye at Trout. Was that a smile he shot back at me?

"That was a very nice thing you did for Evie, son," Mr. Brubaker said and returned his focus to his younger boys.

I nodded again and tapped my fingers on the arms of the chair.

Moments later, Mrs. Brubaker stood in the doorway. "All hail the Christmas Princess."

Evie entered with auburn hair flowing over her shoulders and the biggest grin ever on her face. "Aw, Mom, I'm too old for that princess stuff. But I do feel like one."

"Evie, you look pretty," Mattie said.

"Pwetty," Jacob repeated.

"Thanks, guys." Evie ran to me, threw her arms around my neck, and kissed my cheek.

Face flushed, I patted her on the shoulder and slowly backed away. "I'm glad you like it. But I can't take all the credit. I had a lot of help."

"So that's why you guys all got haircuts," Trout said.

"And that's why Mom insisted on measuring my head," Evie giggled. "I thought she was going to buy me a fancy hat." She stroked her new mane. "It's so much like my hair color."

"Your mom helped with that too." I smiled as she hugged her mother. "I've got to get back home. I promised not to be gone long."

Mr. B. stood, shook my hand again, and said, "We appreciate all you've done. Come back soon."

"Thanks again, Sam." Evie gave me another quick hug before I slipped out the door. As I pulled it shut, a hand grasped it from the inside. Trout stepped out onto the porch with me. "That was a nice thing you did for Evie," he said. The hatred was gone from his eyes. "I won't forget it."

We bumped fists. "Neither will I, Trout."

*****

After supper that evening, BJ, Mom, Dad, and I sat in our usual spots in the living room. The tree lights twinkled. Soft Christmas music played. We reflected on the events of the day. Mom and Dad responded with their usual "being surrounded by those we love" slogan. BJ appreciated the dorm fridge and the new laptop.

I was about to tell them about Evie when the doorbell rang. I jumped up and opened the door. "Trout? Mr. and Mrs. Brubaker, Evie, boys?" I must've sounded pretty stupid.

"For heaven's sakes," Mom said. "Invite them in. It's freezing out there."

"Sorry," I said and motioned for them to come in. Mom joined me at the door, hugging each one as they entered. Dad and BJ greeted them with handshakes.

"Have a seat," Dad said after I made the introductions. Mr. B. sat in Dad's recliner. Mrs. B. rested on the arm of it. Mom and BJ sank into the sofa simultaneously. The rest of the Brubaker family and I plopped on the floor next to the tree.

"It was a nice thing you folks did for our family." Mr. B. broke the silence. "We wanted to personally thank you, especially Sly, for the wonderful Christmas."

"You are certainly welcome," Mom stood again and disappeared into the kitchen.

"Like I was saying, Evie girl, go ahead and tell the pastor."

Evie stood up straight as though she were in the Christmas pageant and cleared her throat. "I just want to thank all of you for the beautiful dress and boots." She looked me square in the eye. "And thanks again Sly for my wig." Her voice cracked like she was going to cry again. And my face heated up...again. Mom returned with a tray of cookies and punch.

Passing the goodies around, Mom said, "What wig? We didn't buy you a wig, dear. Although it looks very lovely. I never would've guessed."

Everyone's gaze turned toward me for an explanation. "The day I delivered the presents, Evie told me she'd be totally bald by Christmas. I came up with the plan and went straight to the gym to ask my friends to cut their hair. We did. Gramps made the wig...not much more to the story. Would you kids like to see a really cool, tiny world?" They all cheered. "Follow me."

Like a parade, we marched upstairs to my room. They took turns admiring the organisms through my microscope, even Trout.

About an hour later, Mr. B. called, "Time to go, kids." They raced down the stairs, shrugged on their coats, said their goodbyes, and left.

The Christmas music filled in the void as I returned to my end of the couch. Again, everyone's gaze fixed on me.

Dad walked over to me, grabbed my hand, pulled me to my feet, and hugged me so tight I thought my ribs would crack. "I'm really proud of you, son...and I owe you an apology. Dave told me about the fights and how you were just defending the smaller kids Grady had been bullying. I'm sorry I never gave you a chance to explain."

Mom and BJ completed the group hug. I felt like a quarter-pounder in a hamburger bun. They finally released me, and we all returned to our usual seats. Slouching, I rested my head on the back of the couch and shut my eyes. Visions of the day ran through my head like the cars in a video game.

I still had a lot to understand about Christmas and God. But the happiness in Evie's eyes, the friendliness in Trout's smile, and the pride on Dad's face taught me all I needed to know about the giving and getting part of the Christmas spirit.

Miss Fabersham's Secret Christmas Gifts

By Cindy O. Herman

"These will be due in two weeks," Susan Zalinski said in her most authoritative, grown-up voice. The seven-year-old opened the front cover on a stack of books at her play table and pulled out the "library card," a slip of white paper tucked inside each book. She inked the due date with a business-like flourish then worked her way through the rest of the books. When she had marked the last card, she snapped the book closed and pushed the stack across the table to her imaginary customer with a crisp, "Thank you. We'll see you in two weeks."

Susan's younger sister, Kimmy, dropped an armload of books on the table and smoothed her skirt—a red cardigan sweater wrapped around her waist—as she sat beside Susan.

"I hope you found everything you were looking for," Kimmy said to another imaginary customer as she opened a discarded reader from their school and reached for her stamper.

Bam. She slapped the stamper on the old inkpad and, bam, stamped a faded "Williams Insurance Co., Inc." on the paper. "Oh, I think your children will like this story. Dick and Jane have quite a few adventures in here."

Bam onto the pad. Bam onto the page. Susan watched Kimmy stamp each book like a real librarian. Lucky Kimmy. She'd found the old stamper in the back of Dad's desk drawer and asked if she could have it. He said yes, and now it was hers.

"Oh, what a lovely choice," Kimmy said to her customer as she stamped Marjorie Majorette, the story of a girl who learned how to twirl a baton and ended up leading a parade through town. It was one of Susan's favorite books. Bam.

"Miss Glenn," Susan said, pushing away from the table and gathering up the books she'd just handled.

"Yes, Miss Watkins?" Kimmy asked.

"I think I'll shelve these books."

Bam. Bam.

"Very good, Miss Watkins. I shall help you as soon as I've finished here." Bam. Bam. "We've been so busy today," she confided to her customer. "Everyone's trying to beat the snow."

Susan's heels—Mom's shoes—clicked as she crossed the floor, her own red cardigan wrapped around her waist. Her two older sisters, Helen and Laura, sprawled on the playroom sofa with a sheaf of construction paper between them. A year apart in age and both with long, dark hair and the brownest of eyes, they were often mistaken for twins. They had decided to create a homemade Christmas this year and were concentrating on folding paper patterns into dozens of colorful, pointy stars. At the far end of the sofa their gray and white cat, Sir Harry, slept. Susan set her books down on the sofa and picked up a purple star.

"Ooh, it's pretty," she breathed, cupping it in her hands and rolling it lightly from palm to palm.

"Don't break it," Laura grumbled.

"Put it down, Sue," Helen, the oldest, said more gently. "They're hard to make."

"Will you show me how?"

"Later," Laura said, concentrating on cutting the paper pattern she'd copied.

"You can help hang them on the tree." Helen's fingers wove and folded strips of deep red construction paper that slowly formed into a star.

"Oh, Miss Watkins?" Kimmy called, pressing the receiver of a toy telephone to her blonde curls.

"Yes, Miss Glenn?" Susan asked, gathering up her books again.

"Could you please see if we have The Little Drummer Boy on the shelf? I have a customer here who'd like to borrow it."

"Let me check," Susan said with a thoughtful frown. She carried her books to the steps, where the girls had lined up every storybook they could find. She stood her armload of books on a step and ran a finger over the spines of another step-full. "Hmm," she mused. Upstairs, she heard Mom walking down the hallway. "Ah, yes. Here it is."

Susan pulled The Little Drummer Boy from the shelf just as Mom started downstairs with a basket of laundry, stepping carefully around the books.

"I just got Eddie down for his nap," Mom said as she reached the last step and entered the playroom. "Just keep the noise down, okay?"

The girls nodded.

Helen held up a star. "What do you think?"

"Nice! They'll look nice on the tree," Mom said.

Helen and Laura smiled.

"Aren't you girls cold without your sweaters on?" Mom asked Susan and Kimmy. "It's cold in here. I'd better check the fire." She hurried by with the laundry and Susan clicked back to the play table.

"Here you are, Miss Glenn."

"Ah, thank you, Miss Watkins," Kimmy said, opening the front cover and reaching for her stamper. Bam. Bam. "It's due in two weeks. I'm sure you'll enjoy it."

Susan looked at Kimmy then the stamper. "Do you think I could borrow that for a while?" she asked.

Kimmy hesitated. "What if I get a customer?"

"Then I could check him out for you." Susan reached for the stamper.

"No." Kimmy slid it closer to herself. "I need it."

"Okay." Susan sighed. "I guess I'll shelve some books."

In the kitchen Susan heard the washing machine start. The cellar door creaked open, and Mom went down into the cellar.

Kimmy pushed her chair back. "Let's set up a Christmas display."

"Yes! Like they had in the library," Susan said. "We'll arrange them on the desk."

The girls hurried to the steps. They started to pull out all the Christmas books just as the front door flung open and their older brother, Joe, raced into the living room, shaking snow off his knit hat. Sir Harry bolted off the sofa and raced upstairs as Joe crossed over the furnace grate in the wide doorway between the two rooms.

"Where's Mom?" Joe asked, pulling off his gloves.

"Fixing the fire," Helen said.

Joe ran through the playroom into the dining room and yelled down the cellar steps, "Mom, can I have a candle?"

Susan heard Mom shaking the metal grate in the furnace, knocking the ashes into the bin. "A candle?" Mom yelled up at Joe.

"Yeah. Someone stole mine, and we're going to race." Joe usually won sled races and was proud of his slick, sanded, and waxed runners.

"Come help me with the coal," Mom called. Joe thumped down the steps in his snow boots, still complaining about the missing candle. In the playroom, the girls looked at each other.

"I thought he waxed his sled last week when it snowed," Kimmy said.

"He did." Helen worked on a yellow star. "He probably just lost it."

A raspy sound echoed as Joe dumped a few shovelfuls of coal into the furnace, talking the whole time with words the girls could not understand. The door clanged shut, and Mom and Joe walked up into the dining room then the playroom.

"Have any of you seen the candle I gave Joe last week for his sled?" Mom asked.

"No," the girls said.

"I left it right on the shelf in the shed." Joe's indignation made his voice rise. "I know I did. Right on the corner next to the sleds."

Mom sighed. "Yesterday it was Eddie's rattle. Now it's the candle." She walked back through the dining room into the kitchen and returned with a small stub of a rose-colored candle.

"Here." She handed it to Joe. "Take this. But don't lose it. And bring it back. It's from the Advent wreath, and that's the one we light this Sunday."

Joe looked at the candle in his hand. "Pink? Don't you have anything else? I can't use a pink candle."

"Take it," Mom said, heading back to the kitchen. "It's the smallest one we have. And bring it right back at supper time."

Joe scowled but pulled his hat back on and ran outside. The girls smiled at each other.

"Well, I'm sure his candle will turn up soon," Kimmy said. "Now we'd better get to our Christmas display, Miss Watkins."

"Oh, yes, Miss Glenn," Susan said. "I'd nearly forgotten in all the excitement."

The two younger girls searched through their "shelves" for the Christmas stories. Helen and Laura worked on their stars, and outside thick white snowflakes floated downward.

*****

That evening after supper, Mom washed the dishes, and Susan and Helen dried and put them away.

"We'll need eighteen bows for the windows," Helen told Mom. "But how many do you think we'll need for the tree?"

Helen's craft magazine lay on the kitchen table, open to the "Happy Homemade Christmas" article. The glossy magazine

105

pictures showed groups of three bows dangling on red and green ribbons in a window.

"Hmm, let me think," Mom said. "I guess it depends on the size of the tree. But probably at least twenty? Maybe thirty?"

"And we'll have other things on it, too," Helen said. "Candy canes…and the Christmas cutout cookies."

Susan dried a dinner plate and put it away in the dining room cupboard. From there she could see Laura at the piano in the playroom practicing A Holly Jolly Christmas over and over again.

"Sounds good, babe," Dad said from the living room, where he sat in his upholstered chair rocking Eddie to sleep and watching Davy Crockett on TV with Joe.

"Thanks, Dad." Laura leaned forward to concentrate on the notes. "Mom got this for me to play on Christmas Eve."

At the play table, Kimmy sat before a pile of papers, an old baby blanket wrapped around her hair and hanging down her back like a nun's veil. She banged the Williams' Insurance Co. stamper into her inkpad and onto one of the papers. Bam. Bam.

"Excellent work, Linda," Kimmy said to a pretend student. "You get a smiling angel with a halo."

She picked up the next paper and frowned. "I don't think you tried very hard on this, Kenny, did you? I'm afraid I have to give you a sad angel."

Susan watched her stamp Kenny's paper with that delightful bam. Planning to join Kimmy in playing teacher after drying the dishes, Susan released a long sigh as she walked back to the kitchen. *But I have to use a red pen to grade my papers.*

*****

After Susan put on her favorite red corduroy jumper and a turtleneck with red and black Scottie dogs, she rushed downstairs. Mom, in a navy blue dress with a white collar and buttons looked pretty, like in her black-and-white wedding photo on the piano. Dad came down pulling on a dark jacket. Light flashed on the gold clasp imprinted with a fancy "Z" Grandpa Zalinski had given him when Dad graduated from high school.

Susan loved Sunday mornings, when the whole family dressed up for church. Her only sorrow was the childish lace veil she and Kimmy had to wear. Mom and the older girls got "real" white veils, but little girls were given doily-type circles of lace to cover just the tops of their heads. Susan held still while Mom bobby-pinned one in her hair, watching with envy as Helen and Laura arranged soft veils over their hair, framing their faces. There was no use complaining. Mom only had three long veils, and she wasn't going to buy a fourth just yet.

At Saint Stanislaus Church, Susan forgot about veils as she drank in the sight and scent of the altar decorated for Christmas. A grouping of fir trees formed a pine-smelling background for the Nativity set, or złobèk, as Mom called it. A statue of Baby Jesus rested in the manger as Mary and Joseph gazed at Him in awe. Shepherds and kings stood nearby.

Maybe we can play with the złobèk when we go home, Susan thought, studying Mary's calm, motherly face. At least that was one game where Kimmy wouldn't need to use her stamp pad.

Back home after church, Susan and Kimmy changed into their everyday clothes and went into the playroom to look in the closet at the family's collection of board games. Mom hurried past on her way to the kitchen, muttering about finding a run in her pantyhose. "I'll have to buy a new pair this week," she said.

Dad rocked Eddie while Laura rummaged through the sheets of music in her piano bench.

"That's funny," Laura muttered.

"Wanna go outside and play?" Kimmy asked Susan.

Susan glanced out at the snow and shook her head. "Not enough time. We'll be eating soon."

"Has anyone seen my holly jolly Christmas music?" Laura called, closing the piano bench lid.

"Nope," everyone said.

"Where did you put it last?" Mom called from the kitchen.

"It was right here. In my bench. Right on top."

"Well, it can't be far," Mom said, peeking into the oven to check on a roasting chicken. "Come help me with dinner. You can pour water in the cups. You too, Helen. Susan, Kimmy, come set the table."

The girls headed for the kitchen, but Laura stopped Susan and Kimmy. "Did you take it? It's not funny if you did. Give it back."

"No," Susan said. "I didn't. Honest."

"Honest," Kimmy echoed.

"Then where can it be?" Laura said. "I need to practice."

"You sounded fine last night," Kimmy said, as the girls opened cupboards and the silverware drawer. "You'll be all right."

Laura seemed to forget about the music as she lit a purple candle in the Advent wreath at dinnertime. Mom and Helen lit two purple candles, and Joe lit a pink one, the same one he'd used to wax his sled runners.

Susan looked over the dancing flames at her family. It will soon be Christmas, she thought with a surge of joy.

After dinner and the dishes, Susan, Kimmy, and Joe pulled on snow pants and boots to go outside. Helen and Laura got out their craft book to make cutout cookie ornaments. Mom wanted to join them, but Eddie wouldn't stop fussing. She hurried into the living room, where Dad was patting Eddie's bottom and crooning a song to him.

"I wish we had his clown rattle," Mom said, picking him up and trying to soothe him. "He loves that."

"Girls, go look in the toy box for Eddie's rattle," Dad said.

"It's not there." Mom snuggled Eddie on her lap. "I emptied it yesterday. I don't know where it is."

Susan shrugged and pulled old plastic bread bags over her shoes before sliding them into snow boots. Kimmy ran to the toy box and rummaged around until she found a brown rubber teddy bear.

"Here, Mommy, try this," she said. "Eddie likes to chew on it."

"Thanks, honey," Mom said, and the children hurried out to play.

*****

Mom usually woke the children up for school, but on Monday morning Susan gradually became aware of voices in Mom and Dad's bedroom. Her eyelids fluttered lazily. Streetlight from outside made the frost on the window panes shimmer like the silver glitter Helen and Laura had glued to some of their paper stars.

"That's not the point," Dad was saying. His voice was low, but he sounded irritated. "I don't mind wearing this one. But where's the other one? It didn't just get up and walk away."

Susan stretched under her quilt and blankets, reveling in the pocket of warmth she'd created.

"It's gotta be here somewhere," Mom said. "I'll find it."

"Well, I've got to run," Dad said. "See you tonight, hon. Love you."

"Love you too. Drive carefully."

Susan heard soft rustling sounds as Mom made the bed and as Dad hurried downstairs. The floor creaked as he walked across the playroom to the closet. She heard the tinny clang of the metal hanger swinging on the closet rod after he yanked his coat free.

If I were a detective, I'd know the man had put his coat on now, Susan thought, remembering the Trixie Belden mystery story she had recently read. She lay still, listening to Dad's steps crossing the living room. When he shut the front door, the wall below her bedroom shook just a little. At the same time, Mom left their bedroom and headed downstairs.

Susan heard the soft crunch of Dad's feet on the walkway in the front yard. Even though the snow was shoveled, his steps sounded different from in the summertime. She heard the click and slam of his car door, and the engine growled to life. Soon his headlights spanned over the bedroom, illuminating Helen and Laura on the bunk beds, and Susan and Kimmy in the "big bed." Susan lifted her chin to catch the beam of light like a luminous kiss and whispered, "Bye, Daddy!"

The room seemed empty when the headlights faded away. Susan slid out of her warm cocoon, grabbed her robe and slippers, and headed downstairs. The playroom and living room were dark. She walked into the light of the dining room just as Mom came out of the cellar, followed by a whiff of hot coals.

"Susan, what are you doing up already? Do you feel all right?" Mom put a hand on Susan's forehead then gave her a kiss and a hug. "No fever. Good morning, Pusta."

The children had always laughed at Busha Zalinski for calling cabbage kapusta, and Mom had ended up teasingly calling them Pusta.

Susan kissed Mom. "Good morning, Mom. I woke up when Dad left, and now I can't sleep."

"It's almost time to get up anyhow," Mom said. "Put your robe and slippers on and come help me get breakfast started."

They set out boxes of cereal, bowls, spoons, bread, butter, and homemade grape jelly. Thrilled to be up before the others, Susan moved briskly, like Mom.

"I can't wait for Christmas," she said.

"I know." Mom sounded more tired than excited.

"What do you think Santa will bring me?"

"Things you like, I hope. But it's more than just getting presents, you know."

"I know," Susan said. "It's about Baby Jesus. But I can't get Him any presents. I'm too young."

"You most certainly can." Mom set milk and a can of Hi-C orange drink on the table. "Hey, get a clean bib out of the drawer for Eddie, will you, please? You can give Baby Jesus all sorts of nice presents. You know that. Tell me what you could give Him."

112

Susan set the bib on the corner of the dining table, near Eddie's high chair, and sighed. "I can help you and Dad…do my homework…and do good in school."

"Those are important things, Pusta." Mom reached out and ran her hand lightly over Susan's hair. "They show that you're thinking of others and doing what you're supposed to be doing. Baby Jesus likes those presents. Right?"

Susan nodded. "But they're not much fun."

Mom chuckled. "I love 'em." She paused, hands on hips, looking at the table. "Okay, we might as well go wake the others."

"Do you think Baby Jesus played with toys, too?" Susan asked as they headed for the stairs. "I mean, when He was a little boy?"

"Oh, I'm sure He did," Mom said. "He also probably liked to play 'teacher,' like you girls do."

"But He was too young to go out and buy anything for Mary and Joseph. So He probably didn't get them presents. Right?"

Mom chuckled softly because they were upstairs now and everyone else was still asleep. "You don't always have to buy something for someone. Maybe Baby Jesus just gave Mary and Joseph a big hug and a kiss and let them know how much he loved them. Sometimes that's the best gift of all. Now go brush your teeth and get your uniform on, and you'll be the first one ready for school."

*****

At breakfast, the children helped themselves to cereal or toast while Mom fed Eddie in the high chair.

"Now I have a serious question to ask," she said, and everyone quieted. "Keep eating, keep eating. You'll be late for school. Dad's tie clasp is missing. He put it on his dresser yesterday after church, and it's gone. Has anyone seen it?"

"No," they all said, looking at each other and shaking their heads.

Mom sighed. "Well, it's got to be up there somewhere."

"Maybe an angel took it to surprise him with it later," Kimmy said.

Mom gave her a curious look, and the others burst out laughing.

"Well, maybe he did," Kimmy said. "It could happen."

"Of course, it could," Mom said. "Now come on, guys. Eat up and get your coats on. It's almost time to go."

*****

When Dad came home that night he said, "Who put that big scratch on top of my car?"

The children looked up from watching Gilligan's Island. There was something about Dad's face. Susan and Joe, sitting on the sofa, turned to kneel on the cushions and look out the window. On the roof of the car lay a Christmas tree!

"You bought a tree!" Joe cried. "The Christmas tree!"

Dad grinned. "We'll decorate it tonight. You girls ready?" He looked at Helen and Laura.

"Yes," they said. "Everything's ready and waiting."

"Good." Dad shrugged out of his coat, headed for the closet in the playroom but then stopped. "Did Mom find my tie clasp?"

"I don't think so," Helen said.

"Well doggone it. I know it was on my dresser. Did any of you kids take it?"

"No." They looked around at each other like they had when Mom had asked that morning.

Dad shook his head and continued into the playroom. "Someone knows what happened to it."

In the living room, the siblings looked at each other.

"He's really mad," Joe said. "Whoever took it better put it back."

"Yeah," Kimmy said.

"I didn't take it," Helen said.

"I didn't, either," Laura said. "And I still haven't found my piano music."

Dad walked into the kitchen.

He talked with Mom while the children listened, having trouble understanding any of their parents' words.

Susan shrugged and turned back to the TV. "It'll turn up."

"Well, it better," Joe said.

"It probably just fell behind the dresser," Susan said. Then she looked at Kimmy, sitting on the floor in front of her. "I can't wait until we decorate the tree. Can you?"

Kimmy stared toward the kitchen.

"Kimmy?"

Kimmy's nerves jumped. "What?"

"Don't you want to decorate the tree?"

"Yeah," Kimmy exclaimed. She glanced toward Mom and Dad, then back at Susan. "Yeah, I sure do!"

*****

After supper, Susan held the front door while Dad and Joe carried the tree into the living room. Susan inhaled deeply, loving the earthy pine scent. Dad had filled a bucket with coal and placed it on the polished wood, two-door cabinet where they kept their puzzles. Dad hoisted the tree up high and plunged it into the bucket. He and Joe twisted and twisted the trunk until it settled into the coal and stood up straight.

"There," Dad said, standing back and looking at Mom. "How's that?"

"Perfect," Mom said. She picked up Eddy, who was crawling on the floor, and put him in the playpen.

Dad winked at Joe, and Joe grinned.

"Lights," Dad said, and Mom handed him a string of colored lights from one of the boxes they'd brought down from the attic. Dad wove the lights among the prickly branches while the rest of the family watched and waited impatiently. Finally, he put the clear plastic star on the top of the tree.

"Ready?" he asked.

"Ready!" they cried.

Dad reached down behind the puzzle cupboard to push the plug into the outlet, and the tree lit up with color all the way to the red-glowing star.

"Yay!" Everyone clapped their hands.

"Yeah, that looks nice." Dad stared at the little tree. "Yup. It's all yours."

He stepped carefully around the Christmas boxes piled in the living room, picked up Eddy, and, because his rocking chair was heaped with boxes, held him on his lap on another lounge chair across the room. Susan stared at the triangle of colored lights on the tree. Even without decorations on it, the lights filled the living room, making it seem warmer and brighter. Susan started to help Joe, Helen, and Laura hang glittery paper bows and colored cutout cookies on the tree. Next she helped Mom unpack the boxes of decorations and put balls, tinsel, and garland in their rightful places. On the living room windows she placed "snow-frosted" red wreaths just above a trio of Christmas bows. On the front door, the colorful, plastic picture of Santa's face encircled by smoke from his pipe. On top of the piano, the red plastic Santa holding an empty sack that Mom always filled with candy canes.

Mom handed Susan a group of wax figurines of boy and girl choir members wearing red robes and white smocks, their little mouths permanently set in O's.

"Put them on the dining table," Mom said.

But Susan was already on her way. "I know," she called excitedly over her shoulder. She set them up in two little rows in the center of the table, just like always, looking like they were caroling on the tablecloth.

As Susan turned to head back for more decorations, Mom walked into the dining room with Helen and Laura.

"I found out what happened to Dad's tie clasp," she said in a low voice. "And your piano music, Laura."

Susan and the girls waited. Mom looked amused, and Susan felt they were about to be let in on a great secret.

"Now, listen, promise you won't say anything to Kimmy about this," Mom said.

Susan glanced at her sisters and nodded. She wondered what Kimmy had to do with the tie clasp.

"Your little sister, God love her, has been taking things and hiding them," Mom continued. "To give to us for Christmas."

"She's giving Dad his tie clasp for Christmas?" Helen asked.

"And Laura's music. Yes. It's her way of going Christmas shopping for everybody. She has a little pile of things all wrapped up and ready to give to each of us. She told me about it after supper tonight because she was afraid Dad would be mad about the tie clasp."

Susan saw the look in Mom's eyes and knew Mom was proud of Kimmy, even while being slightly amused. Susan glanced at Helen and Laura, waiting for their response.

"Oh, how sweet," Helen crooned.

"That Kimmy." Laura grinned.

Susan followed her older sisters' lead. "The little dear." Then, not quite able to hold back her feelings, she added, "But Kimmy's not really giving gifts to anyone, is she? Not if she's just giving us something that's already ours."

"She's giving us something she knows is important to us," Mom said. "She can't buy things for everyone, but she obviously wants to give us something. I think it's very kind and sweet of her."

Susan nodded. "Oh, yeah. Yeah, it is."

"Okay, let's get back to the decorations before she wonders where we are. And remember, not a word."

"I promise," the girls said.

In the living room Susan looked at the red, yellow, blue, and green lights glowing warmly on the Christmas tree. Helen, Laura, and Joe finished hanging candy canes on the branches while Kimmy showed Eddie the figurines from the złobèk.

"And these are the kings," Kimmy said, holding up three little statues in rich robes and crowns. "They brought presents for Baby Jesus. Say 'king,' Eddie."

"Mbah!" Eddie said, reaching for a king.

Kimmy laughed. "No, no, Eddie. They're not for you to play with."

I wonder which of my toys will be missing, Susan thought. What's Kimmy going to give to me?

*****

On Tuesday after school, Susan and Kimmy played librarian again. Their books lined the steps, and they sat at the play table pretending to help one customer after another with crisp flourishes of the pen, on Susan's part, and those official-sounding bams of Kimmy's.

When Susan couldn't stand it anymore she pushed her chair back and stood up saying, "Oh, dear. I'm not entirely certain we have that book, sir. Let me just see."

Sashaying to the steps she ran a finger over the spines of books. Where's my majorette book?

Again, she slowly ran her finger over the books. No, the majorette story wasn't there, and she hadn't seen it in a long time. Aha, she thought and stifled a giggle.

"Oh, Miss Fabersham," Susan called.

"Yes, Miss Weikel?" Kimmy paused, stamper in hand.

"I can't seem to find the majorette book." Susan couldn't stop herself from smiling.

"Marjorie Majorette? Hmm." Kimmy excused herself to her customer and walked over to the steps. "You're sure it's not here?"

"I'm positive."

"Well, perhaps it's been checked out," Kimmy said, stepping back to the play table. "Let me just check the catalog." She rifled through a set of papers on the table and randomly pulled one out. "Ah, yes! Here it is, Miss Weikel." She walked over to Susan and showed her a haphazard list of dates, titles, and the Williamson Insurance Co. stamp. "Marjorie Majorette. It's due back here December twenty-sixth. It should be here right after Christmas."

"Why, that's wonderful," Susan said. "Thank you so much, Miss Fabersham."

"My pleasure." Kimmy returned to the play table and picked up her stamper. "I do apologize for the interruption, madam. Now, where were we?" Bam, bam.

Susan smiled. That's it! That's what she's giving me for Christmas. Oh, the little dear.

*****

Later that night, as the children cleaned up before bedtime, Laura walked into the playroom with Marjorie Majorette.

"Where did you get that?" Susan asked.

"I read it to Eddie tonight." Laura tossed it on the closet shelf with the other books. "He likes it."

Susan put her books away and closed the closet door. Then what did Kimmy take? I haven't noticed anything missing.

*****

The next two days flew by. A winter storm wrapped the house in snow and gave Susan and her siblings a fresh layer for sledding and playing. Helen's craft magazine disappeared and, after looking all over for it, she quietly abandoned the search.

"Oh, Helen, what a shame," Susan said at lunch that day, glancing at Kimmy. "I know how much you love your magazine. I hope it turns up for you soon."

Helen shot Susan a look and said, "I'm sure it will."

Susan watched Kimmy, but her little sister nibbled a cheese sandwich and drank her milk as though oblivious to the conversation.

On Christmas Eve, after Mass, the children put their pajamas and robes on and sat in the living room around the twinkling

Christmas tree. With Mom and Dad, they sang Christmas carols while Laura played along on the piano. She tried A Holly Jolly Christmas, and everyone sang right through the parts she hadn't learned yet.

*****

On Christmas morning, Laura sat up on the bottom bunk and cried, "It's Christmas!"

Susan heard the words as though from far away. She stretched and tried to go back to sleep, but the other girls were waking, too.

"Merry Christmas, everyone!" Kimmy rubbed her eyes and sat up beside Susan.

"Merry Christmas," Helen mumbled from the top bunk.

"Let's go, let's go," Laura urged.

Susan sat up. The sun glared on the snow-covered world outside and seemed to bounce off the walls of their bedroom. "Merry Christmas!"

"All right, all right." Helen sat up at last. She rubbed her eyes and yawned, pushing her long hair out of her face. The girls laughed at her, and she smiled. "Mornin'."

"Let's go!" Laura climbed out from the bottom bunk. Helen slid down from the top, and the four girls padded down the hall to Mom and Dad's room. They stopped in the open doorway. Mom and Dad lay quietly under their blankets. Mom opened her eyes and smiled sleepily.

"Merry Christmas," the girls cried.

"It's not Christmas yet," Dad said, eyes still closed. "You're a day early. Go back to bed."

The girls paused, then laughed and ran to the bed.

"No, we're not! It's Christmas! It's Christmas! Get up, Dad!" They hopped on the bed and pushed at his shoulder. Mom slid out and picked up Eddie, who looked excitedly from face to face.

Joe ran in from his room. "Hey! Merry Christmas, everyone!"

"Let's go downstairs," Susan said.

"Not yet," Dad said. "I don't think anyone brushed their teeth."

Everyone groaned. Dad did this every year, making them wait just a bit longer. They hurried to the bathroom and crowded around the sink to brush quickly. When they got back to Mom and Dad's room, Mom was sitting in bed holding Eddie. Dad still snuggled under the covers.

"Come on, Dad," Joe said.

"Oh, I don't think Santa came this year," Dad said. "Let's just forget it."

"He came! Come on!" the children shouted.

Susan ran to the top of the stairs. She stepped down one, two, three stairs before she could see through the doorway between the playroom and the living room. Standing on the steps, she stared at the tree standing in the corner, colored lights glowing faintly in the sunlit room, surrounded by wrapped packages.

"He came!" she shouted. "He came!"

The other children ran toward her.

"Hey, who's peeking?" Dad called from the bedroom, but he finally got out of bed and walked past everyone toward the bathroom.

"Can we go down?" Susan asked.

"I just have to brush my teeth," Dad said.

The children groaned. "Hurry!"

Finally, Dad came out of the bathroom, Mom carried Eddie, and they all trooped downstairs.

"By golly, Santa did come," Dad said, acting surprised.

The gifts wrapped in bright Christmas paper filled the corner of the room around the puzzle cupboard and were even stacked on one of the chairs. Dad held Eddie and Mom sat near the tree to hand out presents, one at a time, starting with Eddie. It took a long time, and they enjoyed watching each other open presents almost as much as their own, guessing what each gift could be as the paper and bows were ripped away.

Susan got an easel. She'd begged for it after seeing a catalog picture of a girl painting on a paper clipped to the child-sized easel. It had a chalkboard on the other side, where she and Kimmy could play teacher.

Kimmy got a tea set: four metal cups and saucers and a little metal teapot, sugar bowl, and creamer, all painted bright yellow with a red rooster in the center. Everyone glowed with excitement, agreeing that Santa had given them just what they wanted.

"There are a few more presents here," Mom said. From beneath the chair she pulled a small pile of packages, clumsily wrapped with lots of paper and tape. "Kimmy, would you like to hand these out?"

Kimmy beamed as she stood up and waded through piles of gifts and bunched-up wrapping paper. She picked up a package and walked across the room to hand it to Eddie.

"Thanks, babe," Dad said, snatching the present and holding it to his chest, making everyone laugh.

Kimmy giggled. "No, it's for Eddie."

"What? Oh, I'm sorry," Dad said with exaggerated contrition. "Here you go, Ed."

The baby reached for the gift and brought it to his mouth.

"You'd better help him with it," Dad said to Kimmy.

Kimmy pulled the paper away to reveal a rubber clown rattle with a bright yellow, slightly nibbled clown hat and round, red nose. Eddie's smile widened and he stuffed the hat in his mouth.

"How 'bout that? He likes it," Dad said, and everybody laughed.

Laura was delighted to receive her copy of A Holly Jolly Christmas sheet music.

"It's just what I wanted," she said, with a little glance toward Mom, who nodded approvingly.

Helen loved her craft magazine.

"Thanks, Kimmy," she said. "I can't wait to check out their New Year's stuff."

Joe unwrapped his white candle stub. "Great! Now I don't have to use the pink one. Thanks, Kim!"

"You're welcome," Kimmy said grandly.

Mom received a brand new pair of pantyhose, still in its package. "Ooh, thanks," she said, giving Kimmy a kiss. "I need these."

Everyone watched as Dad opened his gift. When he held up the tie clasp with the "Z" on it, the children laughed and clapped.

"Hey, there it is." He hugged and kissed Kimmy. "I'm going to enjoy wearing this again. It's my favorite."

"I know. That's why I gave it to you." Kimmy couldn't have smiled more, and the rest of the family grinned at her and at each other as she hurried back to the chair to bring out one last gift. It was a small box—Eddie's baby shoes could have fit inside. She handed it to Susan and sat down in front of her on the floor. "Merry Christmas."

"Thanks, Kimmy." Susan tugged at the mess of tape, pulled off the wrinkled wrapping paper, opened the lid, and gasped. "The stamp pad!"

She looked at Kimmy, who clapped and laughed.

Susan took the stamp pad and stamper out of the box and held them tightly. "But they're yours."

Kimmy raised her shoulders and laughed again. "Now they're yours."

Susan stared at her. Everyone in the family smiled, and Susan understood something great had happened. She felt the smooth curved handle of the rubber stamper, the cool, rectangular metal of the stamp pad...now hers.

"Thank you," Susan said, feeling how small the words were. She leaned forward and gave her sister a big hug. "Thank you so much, Kimmy!"

"You're welcome," Kimmy said, and it seemed Susan could feel Kimmy smiling through her whole body.

When they relaxed, Kimmy looked from one family member to another then back at Susan. Her little sister had never looked happier. With the tree glittering and every face smiling, Kimmy spread open her arms and cried, "Merry Christmas, everyone!"

"Merry Christmas to you!" they said back, and Mom reached out to hug Kimmy again.

What a great gift, Susan thought, still not quite believing Kimmy could give it up. Susan pictured herself playing teacher, secretary, and librarian, stamping papers with that lofty bam, bam while Kimmy wrote memos and due dates with an ink pen. With a pang Susan realized she never would have thought of doing such a thing for someone else.

You don't have to buy something, Mom had said, to let someone know you love them. It's the thought that really counts.

In a flash, Susan realized how much Kimmy loved her, and the realization glowed warmly in Susan's heart. She reached out and hugged Kimmy once more.

"Thanks, Kimmy," Susan whispered, but she wasn't talking about the stamp pad. "I'm glad you're my sister."

Hobby Horse Faith

By Patricia Souder

George Roe whistled merrily as he stepped off the trolley and headed home. It had been a pleasant Monday of exchanging Christmas greetings with those who called to schedule fuel deliveries at Warren Webster's Heating Firm. Looking down Atlantic Avenue, George noted that the season's first snowfall cast a soft down comforter over his hometown of Collingswood, New Jersey, "the fastest growing community east of the Mississippi River."

As he turned the corner to walk along Knight Park, George gasped at the beauty that surrounded him. Ermine-capped street lights cast their glow over millions of lacey flakes swirling earthward to sprinkle sparkling diamonds over trees, bushes, benches, and walkways in the evening's deepening darkness.

The lustrous snowscapes reminded George of the winter window scenes he and his family had enjoyed at Wanamaker's department store on Saturday and filled him with a fresh sense of hope. Ah, life was good now that he finally had a full-time job again! Especially with Christmas only a week away.

Grateful he'd been able to catch up enough on his bills that he'd felt able to take his family to the newly expanded Wanamaker store for the celebration of its fiftieth anniversary, George wafted his thanks heavenward as he reflected on the massive structure that filled an entire city block and towered twelve floors high!

But when he stepped inside…. Ah! The magnificence of the interior completely eclipsed the magnitude of the exterior.

George closed his eyes to revisit the grandeur of the Grand Court and the glorious music that reverberated throughout the store as thousands of employees and customers thronged the balconies and main floor to sing Christmas carols accompanied by brilliant arrangements on the Great Organ, reported to be the largest in the world.

"George," Nellie had said, "I've heard this is the biggest and most beautiful retail store in the world…and I believe it."

"I do too," George said. "Only it's so awe-inspiring I feel like we're standing in one of the Europe's finest cathedrals."

George took a deep breath. Ah, yes! Wanamaker's Golden Jubilee celebration underscored the incredible growth going on in the Philadelphia area in 1911, a year that had been difficult for George. Now, as he strolled through the snow on his way home, he looked forward to 1912, hoping that it, like the snow-covered world around him, would offer new opportunities.

Deep in thought, George started as a young lady ran toward him, her scarf flapping in the fresh air. She reminded him of Margaret....

Why, it *was* Margaret. What a pleasant surprise!

As she came nearer, she shouted, "Papa, you have to hurry!"

George strode to her side and searched her face. "What's wrong, Margaret?"

"It's Douglas. He's sick. Real sick." Margaret stopped to catch her breath. "Mumsie called the doctor, but she wants you to come home right away."

"Douglas? How can he be sick? He was full of life on Saturday. What happened?"

"I'm not sure. Nana was with him when I got home from school. She seemed worried about his coughing, so I told Mumsie, and Mumsie went up to see what was going on, but when she put her hand on his forehead and listened to his breathing, she ran downstairs and called Dr. Larkin and told me to run find you, so here I am."

"Okay, let's go." George abandoned his memories of Saturday and sprinted through the snow with Margaret.

The minute George opened the back door, he heard a dry, hacking cough and bounded up the stairs where his wife, Nellie, rocked and comforted their five-year-old son.

"He has a fever, George. And he keeps coughing no matter what I do. Dr. Larkin said he'd come as quick as he can, but I'm worried."

George stooped to touch his son's forehead. He certainly couldn't argue with Nellie's assessment.

Douglas reached out his hand and smiled weakly. "I...I'll be okay, Papa. It's...it's just a little hard to breathe," he said between coughs.

George scooped Douglas into his arms, but the boy began coughing more violently than before. George patted his son on the back and pulled a handkerchief out of his own pocket. "Here, son, see if you can cough up whatever's making it so hard to breathe."

Nellie's mother, whom the children called Nana, stared from the far side of the bed as Douglas struggled. "That's how he was when I got so scared," she said.

Nellie got up and put her arm around her mother. "It's good you had Margaret come get me. I hope Dr. Larkin—"

Nellie stopped as Douglas coughed up some watery phlegm and stringy mucus. She noticed Margaret loitering near the doorway, twirling a strand of hair with her left hand, eyes wide with question marks, face distraught. "Margaret," she said, "I want you to go downstairs and wait for Dr. Larkin."

Margaret nodded and left without asking any questions.

Nellie shook her head. "Looks like fear works miracles," she whispered, more to herself than anyone else.

George touched Nellie on the shoulder. "Nellie, don't be so hard on her. She's twelve."

"How well I know," Nellie said, shaking her head wearily. "She usually challenges everything I say."

"Well, maybe she likes her little brother more than she lets on," George said, releasing a hint of a smile.

Nellie shook her head and raised her eyebrows. "Well, that would be nice, George."

Nana walked across the room and stroked Douglas's blond curls. "I don't think he's coughing as much as he was."

"No, he must have fallen asleep," George said. "He feels twenty pounds heavier than when I picked him up."

The three of them breathed a simultaneous sigh of relief, followed by a brief smile as Margaret ushered Dr. Larkin in.

"How's Douglas now?" he asked as he set his black leather bag on a table and took out his stethoscope.

"He seems a little better," Nellie said.

Dr. Larkin felt Douglas's forehead and watched his respirations. "He's breathing pretty fast. Put him on the bed,

George, so I can listen to his heart and lungs and poke around his abdomen."

Douglas winced and groaned. He opened his eyes and tried to push the doctor's hands away until a coughing spasm demanded all his energy.

George, Nellie, and Nana exchanged concerned glances as Dr. Larkin straightened and turned to face them: "Douglas has a severe case of pneumonia. Keep him in bed for two weeks, keep him warm, and see that he gets lots of fluids."

"Pneumonia?" Nellie closed her eyes and shook her head. "That's what I was afraid of." Biting her bottom lip, she wiped tears from her eyes but then rallied. "Doctor, we have to do more than that. Especially when it feels like Douglas is on fire."

Dr. Larkin pulled a brown bottle out of his case and poured about a dozen pills into a small envelope. "Here's some aspirin. Use it only for really high fevers. Don't give him more than one and wait at least four to six hours between doses. Otherwise, sponge him with cool compresses to try to prevent convulsions."

Nellie's face turned ashen, and she looked like she might faint. George reached out to steady her just as Dr. Larkin grabbed a chair and helped her sit. "Mrs. Roe, I didn't mean to scare you. Douglas may not have convulsions. I just thought you should know that it could happen."

Nellie nodded weakly.

"If it does…." Dr. Larkin paused and looked at George and Nana as if he wanted to be sure neither of them was going to faint. "Put pillows around him and protect him so he doesn't hurt himself. You also need two basins of water: one for sponging Douglas and one for washing your hands. And you should burn the cloths he uses to cough up secretions."

Dr. Larkin cleared his throat. "I…I really hope he does well. Douglas has always been one of my favorites. Sturdy. Full of life. Full of questions. Adventurous. But always respectful. He's a fine lad, he is."

Dr. Larkin cleared his throat again and spoke in halted, husky tones. "He'll probably reach a crisis in about a week or so. Then we'll see what the outcome will be. I'll come back next week. But if he gets worse before then, call me."

Nellie pinched her eyes shut to keep the tears from falling, but it was no use. Nana asked quietly, "What about Margaret?"

"Better keep her away from Douglas. Just in case, you know," Dr. Larkin answered. "And the rest of you need to be careful, too."

Douglas stirred, waved his right arm, and smiled weakly as he said, "I'll get better, doctor. It's almost Chris—"

Nellie let out an audible sigh, and Nana helped Douglas sit up as a bout of coughing cut off his sentence.

George walked Dr. Larkin to the door and handed him a dollar bill. "This is all I have today. Let me know how much I owe you, and I'll give it to you when I get my paycheck the end of the week."

"Don't worry about it, George. You have more important things to worry about."

"Thank you so much, doctor. We'll do our best. And we'll pray. A lot."

Dr. Larkin tipped his top hat and stepped into the snow. "Looks like we're getting a white Christmas a week early," he said as placed his black bag on the carriage seat. "And George, I want you to know: I'll be praying, too."

He snapped the reins and called, "Home, Prince. This snow's getting deep."

George reached for his handkerchief before remembering he'd left it in Douglas's room. *"But if he gets worse before then…"* pounded out a cadence of doom.

Tears plunged down his face unbidden. George swiped them with his shirt sleeve, remembering that he and Nellie had waited seven long years to have another child after Margaret had been born. Douglas had filled their lives with joy. But pneumonia was a dreaded foe that claimed the lives of nearly half the young children who contracted the disease.

George choked back his tears, wiped the remaining ones on his other sleeve, and climbed the stairs to rejoin Nellie and her mother. They hugged each other and then looked at the little boy they loved so much.

Nana broke the silence. "This afternoon, he kept trying to tell me about your trip to Philadelphia. 'Ding…ding!' he called as he pulled an imaginary trolley cord. Then he cupped his hands around his mouth and tried to shout, 'Toot! Toot! All aboard!' but it ended in a pathetic croak when he started coughing. A lot. And…well, I wasn't sure what to do."

George put his arm around his mother-in-law. "You did the right thing, Mother Mickle. You had Margaret tell Nellie, and she called the doctor. But, even now, none of us knows exactly what to do."

As George faced the women, he noticed they had dark circles etched under their eyes. "Go rest," he said. "I'll take over for a while. You're both exhausted from a long day."

Nellie hugged her husband. "Thanks, George. I'll bring up some fresh broth and juice before I lie down."

George paced the floor, wondering how to best help Douglas when his son started coughing again. George sat Douglas up in bed and thumped him on the back to help him clear his lungs, catching large amounts of phlegm and mucus in an old handkerchief.

By the time Douglas finished, he was flushed and hot. George dipped a washcloth in the bowl of water on the nightstand and sponged his son in hopes of bringing down his temperature to stave off convulsions.

As he did, he shook his head and asked himself how Douglas had gotten pneumonia. It was all so sudden.

Why, just two days ago, Douglas had been so full of energy, he was up before dawn pitter-pattering through the halls before anyone else was up. George had lain in bed listening, knowing that Douglas would entertain himself safely.

When George got up at seven, he found Douglas sitting on the front porch, already dressed in his favorite outfit: a white sailor shirt with a wide collar and plaid tie, blue knickers over long white stockings, a tunic suit jacket, and a broad-brimmed hat. George watched through the front window as Douglas waved at the milkman, the newspaper boy, and the neighbors who walked by, announcing proudly, "I'm going to Wanamaker's today, and I'll get to ride the trolley and the ferry and maybe even a train."

George smiled as everyone grinned and told Douglas to have a good time. George had no doubt there was something special about his boy. Finally, he opened the door and asked Douglas to set the table for breakfast. Douglas ran in and pointed to the silverware and napkins he'd already placed on the table. "I have it all ready, Papa. Let's eat so we can get going."

"Mumsie and Margaret are coming, too, you know."

"But we have to hurry. We don't want to miss anything."

"Douglas, it's not even 7:30. We have plenty of time."

But Douglas didn't think so and ran upstairs. "Mumsie! Margaret! It's time to eat! Hurry! We don't want to be late."

And so the morning went. After coaxing everyone to hurry, Douglas ran to the Collingswood trolley stop. There he embarrassed Margaret by taking off his hat and waving it grandly as the trolley came into view. The conductor tipped his cap in return, looked at George with twinkling eyes and said, "Well, Sir, you could hire this lad out to the city as a stop sign if you ever fall on hard times."

Douglas's hat-waving worked so well that he repeated it for the captain of the Camden-to-Philadelphia ferry. Then, determined not to miss anything, Douglas worked his way to the front rail where his words rang with delight.

"Oh, Papa, isn't it fun to feel the boat rock?

"Mumsie, listen to the church bells! They're playing the Hark-Angel song!

"Margaret, did you see all those Christmas trees on that big barge?"

At the trolley stop in Philadelphia, Douglas again doffed his hat as the trolley came into view. The conductor waved the Roe family onboard where they were surrounded by talk of Wanamaker's Golden Jubilee, the grand new store, and meeting at the Eagle.

When the conductor announced, "Thirteenth and Market," everyone got out and headed to Wanamaker's.

Bells chimed in the doorways. Chestnuts crackled and popped over open braziers. Window displays featured elves sawing wood and painting toys, reindeer prancing impatiently, and Santa reviewing his list, sometimes nodding approval for those who had been good and sometimes shaking his head and index finger for those who had been naughty.

Other window scenes featured ice skaters making figure eights on a frosty lake surrounded by snow-covered evergreens, carolers dressed in colorful scarves singing under sparkling street lights, children trimming a Christmas tree with strings of popcorn and cranberries, angels singing against a dark blue sky, shepherds rushing to the stable, and Mary and Joseph cradling the baby Jesus. "That's what Christmas is really about, Papa," Douglas had said in awe-struck wonder as he stood transfixed in front of the manger scene.

Douglas had held his father's hand tightly, scrutinizing each scene and commenting on every detail. Margaret, on the other hand, fidgeted, rolled her eyes, scowled, and cleared her throat repeatedly, finally stamping her foot and saying, "We've been here an hour and haven't even gone in the store. How am I going to find a new Christmas outfit and the right jewelry to go with it?"

Nellie started to correct her but George intervened. "Nellie, take Margaret and go ahead. Meet us at the Eagle in the Grand Court at quarter of twelve so we don't miss the music."

George and Douglas continued to examine each window scene until the Great Organ began playing. George tapped Douglas on the shoulder and led him inside.

Thousands of clerks and customers had already gathered on the marble floor and in the upper level galleries to sing Christmas carols by the time George and Douglas entered Wanamaker's massive doors.

"Papa, I never saw anything so big or beautiful," Douglas said, eyes so wide with wonder they took up most of his cherubic face.

And when Douglas joined in singing "Away in a Manger," George choked back tears as he remembered the clarity and sincerity in Douglas's voice.

Was that really only two days ago?

A heart-wrenching sound brought George back to the present. Douglas was coughing violently and struggling to breathe. George sat him up, thumped his back to loosen the secretions, and helped him cough up mucus that was thicker and darker than before. Douglas breathed a little easier, but his respirations were still rapid and shallow, and he felt flaming hot.

Douglas pointed to his chest. "It hurts, Papa."

George nodded. "I know, son. That's because you're sick. Dr. Larkin says you need to take this little pill and drink lots of water and juice so you get better. Do you think you can do that?"

"I'll try, Papa," Douglas said, sipping juice as George placed the pill on the boy's tongue. Douglas made an awful face as he tried to swallow the pill. Then he cried, "Ach—Ach!" and pointed to the back of his throat. "Tuck!" he forced out. "Tuck!"

George grabbed a glass of water and held it to Douglas's lips. "Drink, Douglas, drink! Drink so the pill dissolves and you can breathe again."

Douglas tried to drink, but the water ran out of his mouth, and he turned blue while grasping his throat and trying to spit out the pill. George sat Douglas up and pounded his back, praying, "Dear God, please help Douglas breathe again."

As if in answer to that prayer, Douglas finally started coughing. Juice, blood-tinged mucus, and the half-dissolved pill flew out of his mouth.

"Thank You, God!" George cried, choking back tears with every word.

Douglas nodded and tried to smile, but made a sour face and pointed to the back of his throat. "I...I can breathe again, Daddy...but it still tastes bad."

George hugged his son and offered him some water. Douglas drank a little but shook his head and scrunched up his face again.

"Still bad?" George asked.

Douglas nodded.

"I'm really sorry. When you're breathing okay, I'll go find something to take away that nasty taste."

Douglas grimaced and pointed to his throat. "Now!" he said, his voice weak but his intent clear as he lay back on the pillow.

George squeezed his son's shoulder gently. "Okay, Douglas. You rest, and I'll be right back."

George took the back stairs to the kitchen where he found Nellie preparing a plate of food.

"Oh George, I'm so glad you finally came down for supper."

"I can't stop for supper. I have to get something to take away the bad taste in Douglas's mouth. I should have cut up that pill, but I didn't, and it got caught in the back of his throat, and he nearly choked, and—"

Nellie put her finger over George's mouth. "I know. I heard and came up to help, but Douglas had just coughed up the pill, so I came back down and dished out some gelatin for him. And some supper for you. You haven't had a thing to eat, and it's almost time for you to go to bed, so sit down and eat."

"It's hard to take time to eat when Douglas is so sick."

"I know. But if we don't take care of ourselves, there won't be anyone to take care of Douglas."

"You're right, Nellie. But I don't want anything to happen to him."

"None of us do." Nellie picked up the gelatin, brushed back a few tears, and headed upstairs.

George ate quickly and rejoined Nellie in Douglas's room.

"Papa, remember—" Douglas sat up and coughed.

"Oh, Douglas—" Nellie patted his back to loosen his secretions.

Douglas coughed up more thick, blood-tinged mucus and then lay back on his pillow. Although exhausted, he muttered, "Choo…Choo…."

George ran his fingers through Douglas's hair. "Oh, you're thinking of the trains in the Toy Department, aren't you?"

Douglas nodded.

George turned to Nellie. "Well, Mumsie, you should have been with us! Douglas was the finest of engineers. He made friends with the man in charge of the trains as soon as we got there, so the man let Douglas throw the switch to make the locomotives puff steam and toot whistles while the trains climbed the trestles and crawled through the tunnels."

Douglas sat up, a faint sparkle in his eyes. "The…village…."

"Oh, yes, Douglas loved the village with its miniature people and the snow-covered trees and houses and stores and churches."

"And little dogs and street lamps." Douglas tried to smile but another coughing spell consumed all his energy.

"It's all right, Douglas," George said. "We can talk about it another time."

Douglas shook his head. "I want Mumsie to know—"

Nellie helped Douglas with his coughing while George tried to figure out what their son meant. "About the train station? You sure enjoyed flipping the switches to make the red and green lights flash and the gates go up and down."

Douglas nodded but then shook his head again.

"Do you mean the building blocks?" Douglas shook his head no. "The wooden soldiers? The spinning tops? The Tinker Toys?"

Again Douglas shook his head and seemed to grow more frustrated with each new suggestion. He patted his throat as if it hurt and began to rock back and forth slowly. "Rock...rock...." he whispered weakly.

"Oh, yes," George said. "You want Mumsie to know about the hobby horse, don't you?"

Douglas nodded.

George cleared his throat. "Well, it was a beauty, Mumsie. A dappled silver white horse with real pony hair for its mane and tail. It had curved rockers with a sturdy platform for mounting." George stopped and swallowed. Douglas smiled broadly and rocked back and forth.

"Yes...." George hesitated. "Well, Douglas really liked rocking on that horse."

"I love that horse, Papa," Douglas said, blue eyes luminous and longing. He massaged his throat and then whispered between rapid breaths, "I don't want...any other toys...but I...would really...love...to have...that horse...for Christmas."

George swallowed again and tousled Douglas's hair. Then, as if Douglas had accomplished his mission, the little boy fell asleep, a slight smile turning up the corners of his mouth.

George took a deep breath. "Well, Nellie, now you know. Douglas was mesmerized by that horse. He loved playing with the trains, so I thought sure he'd want a train set, but he never asked for that. It's as if he knew we couldn't afford it. He liked building a tower with the building blocks, spinning the red musical top on display, and arranging the wooden soldiers in platoons.

"But when he spotted that hobby horse in the back corner. Oh, Nellie, it was a love affair! He stood and gazed at the horse, his eyes sparkling with delight and his mouth open in awe. After a few minutes, I leaned down and told him he could ride the horse if he wanted to because Wanamaker's allows children to play with the toys on display.

"Douglas climbed on and rocked for twenty minutes. By then, three children were waiting for a turn. I pointed to the children and told Douglas he'd have to stop...even though I was convinced the other children might never have noticed the horse if they hadn't seen Douglas enjoying it so much."

George shook his head and took a deep breath. "Nellie, I'm sure it doesn't look like a big present to him, but when I turned over the price tag...there's no way we can afford to buy that horse for him."

George sighed and his shoulders slumped. "I can't stop thinking about it, and I keep wishing...."

Nellie put her arm around George's waist and guided him to the door. "You can't let that consume you, George." She stood on tiptoe and kissed him. "You have to get up early in the morning to go to work, so Mother and I will take turns caring for Douglas tonight. And...well, we'll just have to trust God to work everything out."

George nodded and tipped Nellie's head up so they were looking directly into each other's eyes. "You're right again, Nellie, but I hate to have you and your mother stay up all night."

"There's no other choice, George."

*****

The days leading up to Christmas left little room for arbitrary choices. George worked long hours in the office of Warren Webster's Heating Firm as customers stocked up on fuel for the holidays. Nellie and her mother took turns cleaning, decorating, and baking to preserve the family's most treasured Christmas traditions, but most of their time was devoted to caring for Douglas.

Margaret studied hard for her pre-Christmas exams and memorized her lines for the Christmas pageant, but she frequently found excuses to go upstairs and peek into Douglas's room even though she normally tried to distance herself from her bothersome little brother.

Worried that Margaret might also come down with pneumonia, Nellie constantly looked for ways to keep her away from Douglas's room.

"Margaret, I need you to go to the store and get sugar." Or flour. Or milk. Or eggs.

"Margaret, I need your help in hanging the garland over the door."

"Margaret, if we're going to have any Christmas cookies, you'll have to help bake and decorate them."

Margaret grumbled that she was always working, but overall, she cooperated more than usual.

Douglas continued to run high fevers with frequent coughing spells producing thick, rusty sputum. Keeping him hydrated demanded creativity and perseverance because nothing tasted good to him, his throat hurt, his fever dehydrated him, and he drowsed off frequently. When he was awake and not coughing, however, he heard the activity downstairs, smelled the cookies baking, and listened to the family talk about Christmas activities, letting whoever was caring for him know that he missed being part of it:

"Oh, Mumsie, you know how much I love making Christmas cookies.

"Nana, I'm the one who always sets up the nativity set.

"Papa, I love holding your hand while we go Christmas caroling.

"Margaret, will you hang up my stocking?"

They all did their best to encourage Douglas and entertain him while silently suppressing tears, knowing no one loved Christmas more than Douglas.

Margaret built a snowman where Douglas could see it from his window and hung a jolly elf on his door. One day she tried to sneak a Christmas cookie to him, but her grandmother intercepted her.

"Margaret," Nana said softly, "what a nice idea! Except, honey, the crumbs might get caught in your brother's throat, and then what would happen? Besides—"

"I know. I'm not supposed to be here." Margaret grimaced, wrapped the cookie back in its napkin, and stuffed it in her pocket, glad it was Nana who'd caught her instead of Mumsie.

Nana brought Douglas a Christmas coloring book and told him stories to go with the pictures. When Douglas felt well enough, he sat up and colored the pictures.

Mumsie helped Douglas cut out a manger scene from thin cardboard and then painted it and arranged it on his dresser. Douglas made a game out of pointing to the figures and making Mumsie guess which one he wanted her to touch so he could say who they were: "Mary...Joseph...Baby Jesus...Shepherds...Little Lamb...Baby Jesus."

George discovered that singing Christmas carols helped soothe his son in the evenings. Douglas was usually too weak to join in, but once in a while, he sang a line or two, his voice ragged and discordant, rather than pure and angelic like it had been in the Grand Court on Saturday.

Almost every night, Douglas rocked back and forth, saying "rock...rock" over and over. Then, when he could rock no more, he lay back on his bed and said with great certainty, "Oh, Papa, I know that horse will be under the tree."

The question of the hobby horse and the little boy's faith hovered near the edge of consciousness like rain clouds on an overcast day. "What will we do, Nellie?" George asked. "He won't take no for an answer."

Nellie shook her head and shrugged her shoulders.

"How could I have known he'd ask for a hobby horse? He might just as well have asked for the moon."

"I know," Nellie said, a great sigh welling up inside. "I can't bear to think how disappointed he'll be when that hobby horse isn't under the Christmas tree. It's hard enough for a little boy who loves Christmas to be so sick with pneumonia so that he can't get out of bed until New Year's Day. Yet he seems to have accepted that. 'Well, then,' he told me, 'we'll just have Christmas a week late.'"

George put his arm around his wife. "He's really growing up, isn't he? I wish we could make him understand about the hobby horse."

"Me too. But George, he really believes it will be there."

"I know, Nellie, I know," George said, his voice flat with discouragement.

*****

Douglas's words haunted George. He wanted desperately to buy Douglas the prized hobby horse, but he was still behind financially. It would be foolish to even consider it. He and Nellie had already agreed to give up Christmas presents for each other so Margaret and Douglas could have gifts. But there was no way they could afford the hobby horse that Douglas wanted.

Work was especially busy on Saturday. Dozens of people called to make sure their fuel would be delivered before Christmas and to ask other assorted questions. By the time George finished work, dark clouds hovered ominously outside. He closed his eyes, almost too weary from the week's heavy workload and constant worry to get up and put on his jacket.

The firm's owner stopped George as he reached for the doorknob to leave.

"Here, George," he said, handing him an envelope. "I want you to have this. Thanks for all your hard work. Merry Christmas. And I hope your son gets better soon."

"Thank you, Mr. Webster," George said, reaching to shake his boss's hand. "I really appreciate your good wishes...and this job. It means a lot to me."

George pulled up the collar on his jacket against the wind as he sloshed through the murky slush created by the partially melted snow and the icy sleet slicing through the sky. Tired as he was, he picked up his pace. He couldn't afford to miss the trolley on a night like this.

*****

George's feet were soaked long before he got home. He pulled off his shoes and put them on the mat inside the door. His feet felt like blocks of ice. He placed his soggy hat on the hat rack and wandered into the kitchen before hanging up his jacket. "Nellie, I'm home."

"George, you're drenched!" his wife said as she looked up from the pot she was stirring at the stove. "Good thing I decided to make chicken noodle soup. Douglas isn't the only one who's going to need it."

"It's nasty out there," George said as he walked toward Nellie to give her a hug.

154

Nellie backed away, saying, "George! Go hang up that dripping jacket and dry off!"

George peeled off his jacket and hung it on the coat tree. As he did, he felt the envelope Mr. Webster had given him poke out of his shirt pocket. "I almost forgot about this," he said, returning to the kitchen to show Nellie the envelope. "Mr. Webster gave this to me just before I left the office."

Nellie stopped stirring and said, "Well, let's open it."

When they did, a check fell out. George picked it up, and when they saw the amount, they both gasped. "Oh, George, isn't that wonderful?" Nellie cried. "Your bonus will help pay off most of our bills."

George nodded as his eyes teared up with gratitude. "You're right, Nellie, just like usual. But...this check's just about half as much as that hobby horse Douglas wants." George paused. "Do you suppose the horse will still be there next week?

Nellie threw herself into George's arms and wept long-suppressed sobs. "Oh, George, I just hope Douglas will still be here next week."

*****

Sunday dawned clear and cold. George got up early and put on his boots to shovel the icy-snow mix on the sidewalks. He felt a slight tickle in his throat.

"Maybe I should stay home from church with Douglas." He cleared his throat as he came in.

"You'll do no such thing," Nellie said. "You've been practicing for your solo for months. I'll warm up some soup for you."

"For breakfast?"

"You have a solo, George."

"I know. And that's what I'm worried about. Besides, you and your mother have taken care of Douglas all week."

"You'll do fine with your solo, and you'll get your turn with Douglas this afternoon and all day tomorrow." Nellie poured soup into a pot and filled the teakettle with water. "Be sure to take Margaret with you. No reason for her to sit around here glumming over everything."

George smiled. "Glumming? Nellie, that's not a word."

Nellie faced him, hands on her hips. "Oh, you know what I—"

"Never mind," George said, smiling. "I'm on my way upstairs to see how Margaret's coming along while you heat the soup."

Margaret, still in her nightgown and robe, turned from looking out her bedroom window as her father called her name from the doorway. She argued against going to the service, saying it wasn't fair to go when Douglas was home sick because he was the one who loved "Christmas church."

George countered that Douglas loved everything about Christmas, no matter what it was, and that Douglas was not the issue. In the end, Margaret agreed to go if she could wear her new outfit.

"But you won't have anything under the tree tomorrow morning," George warned.

"So who wants presents under the tree when nobody's there to open them anyway?" Margaret said, her bottom lip quivering.

"Margaret," George said, pulling her close. "You really miss Douglas, don't you?"

*****

Margaret linked arms with her father to keep her balance on the slippery sidewalks as they walked along Park Avenue to the Collingswood Methodist Church. "Maybe I should have worn boots like you," she said as they encountered an unusually slick spot.

"Maybe. But we're almost there now. Just hang onto my arm and be careful," George said, thinking how much she reminded him of Nellie. "It should be melted by the time we go home."

"It's so different from last week," Margaret said slowly. "It...it just doesn't seem like Christmas Eve."

George nodded and patted Margaret's arm as they neared the church. Families bustled about calling "Merry Christmas!" as they greeted one another.

"You'll be okay while I sing in the choir, won't you?" George asked.

"Of course. I'm a big girl now, you know," Margaret quipped.

But George detected a slight catch in her voice.

*****

Congregational carols and Christmas scriptures filled the early part of the service. George found it difficult to sing "Joy to the World" as he thought of Douglas's struggle to stay alive...until the words of the third stanza caught his attention:

"No more let sins and sorrows grow,

Nor thorns infest the ground;

He comes to make his blessings flow

Far as the curse is found,

Far as the curse is found,

Far as, far as the curse is found."

That's it! George thought. *It isn't just Douglas but the whole world that's struggling under sin's cruel curse. The joy of Christmas is that Christ came to break that curse and bring eternal blessings to everyone!*

George sang the fourth stanza with strength, re-energized in spirit and grateful for the chicken soup and the hot lemon and honey water Nellie had given him for breakfast.

He cleared his throat as the Chancel Choir rose to sing Christmas selections from *The Messiah*. The organ's sonorous introduction gave him courage to sing the opening solo with compassion and warmth: "Comfort ye, comfort ye my people…" after which he sang the tenor aria that followed with confidence and joy: "Ev'ry valley shall be exalted . . . and ev'ry mountain and hill made low…."

George felt like a new man as he left the choir loft to find Margaret.

"Oh, Papa, you've never sung so beautifully!" she said, stretching up to kiss him on the cheek. "I've heard you sing many times. And I've heard you practice, too. But this was the best! It was marvelous! I'm so glad you made me come."

George was speechless. Margaret had never cared about music before, and she frequently argued about going to church.

Why, this is a Christmas miracle! George thought.

"You're not going to faint, are you, Papa?" Margaret asked, a slight smile playing at the edges of her mouth.

"I hope not, Margaret," George said, a warm twinkle in his eyes. "But it means a lot to hear you say that."

"Papa, what's going to happen to Douglas?" Margaret's voice quivered.

George cleared his throat and stroked the side of his face. "I wish I knew, Margaret. But at least I've been reminded that Christ came to comfort his people and to eventually put an end to all the problems that plague us."

"Eventually's not soon enough for Douglas," Margaret said, tears flooding her eyes.

George nodded in agreement and put his arm around Margaret as they walked out of the church.

*****

George spent the entire afternoon with Douglas, who was still plagued by frequent coughing spells and a fever. Although weak and thin, he seemed to be more alert than he'd been. He even beat George at a game of checkers which made both of them chuckle.

Margaret coaxed her mother into going for a walk. It was the first time Nellie had been outdoors in a week. When they returned with their arms full of holly and evergreen boughs, Nellie sent Margaret upstairs to see if Nana would also like to get a little fresh air.

That evening, Nellie insisted that everyone sit down to have Christmas Eve supper together as Douglas seemed much better and had fallen asleep. Margaret placed a centerpiece of fresh greens on the table she and Nana had arranged, along with gold napkins

160

folded into stars. George thanked God for the food and prayed for Douglas's healing.

After supper, Nellie gave each of them a candle and turned out the lights while they sang "Silent Night." Just as they finished, a bell tinkled from Douglas's bedroom.

George took the stairs two at a time, eager to find out what Douglas needed. Douglas was awake, but groaning. His breathing was more rapid than earlier, and he whimpered, "Hurt!" as he pointed to his throat and his abdomen.

George felt his forehead. It was certainly hotter than earlier that afternoon. "Nellie!" he called, but she was already at the doorway. "Bring me some cool water. We need to sponge him."

George, Nellie, and Nana took turns sponging Douglas all evening. Despite their efforts, Douglas's temperature kept climbing. He lapsed in and out of consciousness, often mumbling disconnected words and phrases. "Don't you think we should call Dr. Larkin?" Nellie asked.

"I hate to call him on Christmas Eve," George replied.

"But he said to call if Douglas got worse, and he's definitely worse," Nellie said, panic straining her voice.

"Yes," George agreed, "he's worse. But it's strange because he was so much better this afternoon." Puzzled, George shook his head. "All right, you stay with Douglas, and I'll go call."

No one answered even though the phone rang many times. "I think he may have gone away for Christmas," the operator said as she disconnected the call. "Do you want me to try someone else?"

While George tried to think what to do, Nellie shrieked, "George!"

George could hear that Douglas was having convulsions before reaching the room. "Hand me a pillow to protect his head. Put another between him and the wall. Hold another on this side of the bed so he can't fall out."

No one clocked the convulsions, but it seemed as if they would never stop. By the time they did, Douglas was soaked with perspiration, and George and Nellie were exhausted.

Nana stood at the door. "I think that was the crisis," she said. "I'll help you change Douglas and his sheets, and then I'll stay with him while you rest."

Nellie looked at her mother in wonder. "How do you know that was the crisis?"

Nana smiled. "I had children once."

"Does this mean he'll get better?" Nellie asked.

"You did," her mother answered, giving Nellie a squeeze.

*****

The Roes celebrated Christmas quietly but with fresh hope that Douglas would recover. His coughing became less frequent, and his fever broke. He slept for long periods, and when he woke, his mind was clear. He drank large amounts of juice and broth and soon began asking for something to eat.

*****

Dr. Larkin came Tuesday morning.

"Well, Douglas looks much better," he said as he listened to Douglas's chest and Nellie's rendition of the crisis. "I'm sorry I wasn't home. I had no way of knowing when the crisis would come. We got a call that my father was sick, so we went to see him for Christmas.

"But really, you did everything right. There's nothing I could have done any better. And now that Douglas is past the crisis, it's a matter of building up his strength with nourishing drinks and foods.

"Keep him in bed until New Year's Day. Then you can carry him downstairs and let him walk around a bit. Gradually, day by day, he'll get better."

*****

George had gone back to work on Tuesday, but business between Christmas and New Year's Day was so slow that Mr. Webster told George to go home early on Friday.

George took the ferry to Philadelphia and headed straight to Wanamaker's toy department, Douglas's strong faith propelling him forward as he heard Douglas say, "It will be there, Papa. I know it will."

Hardly able to breathe, George prayed in a way he'd never done before. "Please Lord, let Douglas's hobby horse still be there…and at a price I can afford."

George found the toy department eerily empty. A sales clerk asked if she could help, and George explained his plight.

"Hobby horses were very popular this year," the clerk said. "I don't think there are any left."

George's shoulders drooped and he swallowed hard. When he told the clerk of Douglas's love affair with the dappled silver white horse, she rubbed her chin and wrinkled her forehead as if in deep thought. "Well, I don't want you to get your hopes up, but I'd like to check the stockroom."

The clerk returned with the very horse Douglas loved. "This was our floor model, so we put it in the back because the paint is chipped on the platform and the rockers where the children got on and off the horse. If you're willing to take it as is, I can sell it to you for a good price." She smiled. "A very good price."

George listened to the figure in amazement. It was only a third of the ticket price! "I can afford that, Ma'am. Thank you. Thank you very much. You'll never know how much this means!"

*****

George cradled the treasured horse in his arms as he took it home via ferry and trolley. The next day, he found some paint to touch up the scuffed spots on the platform and rockers. Nellie made a big red bow which George tied around the horse's neck.

Nellie and Margaret spent the afternoon making hobby horse sugar cookies for Douglas. George smiled to himself as he listened to their chatter and laughter as they tried to outdo each other in creating horses with distinctive personalities by the way they shaped and decorated the cookies.

Nana volunteered to stay home with Douglas on Sunday so she could make him his favorite custard. That afternoon, everyone took turns reading and playing games with Douglas, whose main topic of conversation was his excitement about going downstairs on New Year's Day to ride his hobby horse.

Margaret asked him if he wished he could right then. "No, I've waited this long. I'm looking forward to having Christmas on New Year's Day, and I'm not going to spoil it now."

That evening, Nellie fixed a platter of tea sandwiches and gathered everyone together to have a New Year's Eve picnic in Douglas's room. George asked each of them to tell what was the highlight of the year, but when everyone said it was Douglas's recovery, he had them join hands and form a circle to thank God as a family .

Once Douglas was tucked in for the night, Nana wrapped the nativity set figures and put them back in their box so Douglas could set them up the next day. Margaret filled Douglas's stocking with an orange and an apple, candy, nuts, a tiny train, and a box of colored pencils that she prized.

On New Year's Day, George sang "Joy to the World!" as he carried Douglas downstairs. As they entered the living room, everyone shouted, "Merry Christmas!"

Douglas looked at the Christmas tree from his father's shoulders and cried, "See! My hobby horse! Right there by the tree! I knew it! I knew it would be there!"

And then, having waited so long, Douglas wriggled out of his George's arms and climbed on his longed-for steed and rocked in rapture.

Margaret, Nana, Mumsie, and Papa looked on in wonder, tasting tears of joy as they watched the little boy who'd survived a Christmas crisis herald in a new year filled with hope.

The Christmas Letters

By Shirley Leonard

"You wrote a letter for a Christmas present? Seriously, Grandma? That's so lame. But then, I shouldn't be a critic. I have no clue what to do for Christmas this year myself."

Fourteen-year-old Abby was off from school since it was a teachers' in-service day, so she'd come over early to help. The feisty redhead opened yet another sturdy carton and sighed. "Nope, they're not in here either."

Rose shifted in her power wheelchair and smiled tenderly at her youngest granddaughter. "Maybe we'd better give this a rest for now, honey. It's getting close to lunch time, and I don't know about you, but I could use a break."

While Abby had been searching through boxes she'd carried down from the attic of the old farmhouse, Rose had been lovingly packing her best china. Her beloved heirlooms would soon find a new home with Abby's older sister, Megan, a newlywed. That was a happy thought.

Rose Thomas needed all the happy thoughts she could find. Only three weeks were left before her move into an apartment in Lake View Manor. The big old house had been fine until a stroke landed her in a wheelchair. Her son-in-law added ramps outside and made adjustments where he could inside, and for a long while, it worked. But the upstairs was just wasted space now, and she knew that life would be much simpler in the first floor unit at Lake View. She had friends who'd lived there for years and loved it, and Rose admired the lovely apartments. She'd prayed about this move long and hard. But downsizing was daunting, emotionally as well as physically. She was grateful for everything her family was helping her with. Sort of.

They all meant well, but sometimes Rose felt trapped. She was an emotional wishbone. Precious memories pulled at her to linger. Her daughters pushed her to hurry and toss out anything she couldn't use in the new apartment. She wanted to be practical, but the Christmas letters....

The phone interrupted Rose's train of thought, and Abby ran to answer it.

"Thomas residence. Abby speaking."

Rose smirked at the formality, recalling how this dramatic teen had done a job-shadow week at the school where her Aunt Karen taught and that she spent a lot of time in the office with the receptionist.

"Yes, she's right here. May I tell her who's calling?"

Abby's hand covered the receiver as if she were on a covert mission. "It's somebody with a deep voice named Phillip, Grandma. What's up with that?"

"Give me the phone, young lady, and how about warming up the leftover chowder from last night?"

Abby rolled her eyes but handed over the phone and sauntered out to the kitchen.

"Hi, Phil. Yes, Abby's been here all morning. We're making progress but still haven't found the Christmas letters. I'm starting to wonder if I really saved them or just thought I did. Sure, I'd love to go to the concert next week. See you then. Bye."

"Grandma, you have a date? Is he hot?"

"Oh, Abby. What will I do with you?"

"Keep feeding me your scrumptious molasses cookies, and I'll be your slave forever."

"That's a deal. After chowder we'll have cookies. Let's eat."

When they finished eating, Abby rinsed the dishes and loaded them into the dishwasher, whistling a tune Rose didn't recognize.

"What's that melody, Abby? I don't think I've ever heard it."

"I'm not surprised, Grandma. It was a YouTube hit that went viral quite a while back called 'What Does the Fox Say?' Do you want to watch it with me? I can get it on my IPod in a jiff."

"Sure. Why not?"

Soon both Rose and Abby were laughing out loud at the silly song and sillier video. "Wait a minute. That makes me think of something. There's a trunk in the corner of the attic with a fake fox stole and other old props from the drama club I belonged to. When we disbanded, nobody else wanted the stuff, so they just gave it all to me. Your mom and aunts used to get those things out when they played dress-up. I think I may have tucked a long box under the stole in the trunk. Will you go up and see if you can find it?"

"Sure, Grandma. This is starting to feel like a scavenger hunt. I didn't expect to have this much fun helping you get ready to move." Abby ran up the stairs, blowing Rose a kiss as she went.

Pushing the button on her power chair, Rose maneuvered herself back into the den and settled in beside the gas fireplace. How she'd miss this cozy room.
Soon she heard Abby's footsteps plodding slowly down the stairs, and her heart sank. She must have been wrong about where that special box was stored, or Abby would have rushed back down with excitement.

"Grandma, I think this is it. I feel like I'm holding a piece of history or something. Look.

The box is even labeled The Christmas Letters." Abby tenderly placed the lovely box on Rose's lap and waited. Rose suddenly realized Abby's deliberate descent on the stairway was the result of the girl just now recognizing the significance of her discovery.

With misty eyes, Rose held the box. "Oh, honey, you found it. Now let's see if the letters are still in one piece. They've been up there a long time."

"Do you want me to scram, Gram? I mean… these are your personal letters, after all, and if you want to read them by yourself, I totally get it."

"No, honey. I want to share them with you. I need to have somebody else here so I can fill in the gaps and tell you some of the back story. Are you up for that?"

"Sure. Mom won't be here to pick me up for an hour or so. Will that be enough time?"

"Well, it'll be a chance to start anyway. Here goes."

Rose carefully untied the gold ribbon from around the box and lifted out the first letter. It was short and written in longhand on heavy vellum with a lovely hand-painted border of holly glued to red construction paper.

*****

Christmas 1968

Dear Mom and Dad,

173

On this, our first Christmas since our wedding, David and I were hoping we'd be able to give you something very special. You have done so much and deserve an elegant gift. But since money is tight, and we used what we had for gas to come home, the gift we have for you isn't anything we bought. Instead, our gift is the news that sometime in late July, we will present you with your first grandchild.

All our love,
Rose and David

*****

"Wow, Grandma. Now I get it. That letter wasn't lame at all. Tell me about how you decided to write it."

The years rolled away in Rose's mind as she took Abby's hand and squeezed it. "How would you like to make us both a cup of tea? That'll give me a chance to collect my thoughts."

"Sure, Gram. Tea sounds good."

Soon Abby was back, and as she held the warm cup, inhaling the soothing chamomile blend, Rose thanked God for the chance to finally share these memories. Taking a long sip of tea and then a deep breath, she just let the thoughts pour out.

"It was 1967, and we were so young and in so love and so— broke. Christmas was coming soon, and I started to panic. What in the world could I give my parents that first Christmas after our wedding? It had to be something special so they'd know how much they meant to me. Then I thought about how many cows

Dad had to milk on our farm in New York, and how many hours Mom spent on her feet at the restaurant to make college possible for me. Who knew that I'd meet your Grandpa David there and fall hopelessly in love, get married, and live in Pennsylvania happily ever after? It's not like I deserted them on purpose, but that's how it felt, so I wanted to give them something wonderful.

"But what could I do with no money for gifts? I had to get creative, and so I wrote them that letter. You thought it sounded lame, and, believe me, it felt lame at the time. But when my parents, your great-grandparents read it, we all cried happy tears. And suddenly my gift didn't feel lame after all."

"That's awesome, Grandma. So—that was the news about Aunt Karen, right?"

"Right. And that's how the tradition of the Christmas letters began. Of course, back then I had no idea of starting a tradition. It just sort of happened. Some of the letters I wrote, and other letters family members wrote to me or to each other. "

"Hey, anybody home?" Abby's mom, Beth, scurried in, with windblown hair dusted with snow. "I thought you two were working on packing? This looks like goofing off to me."

"Hi, Mom," Abby said. "Guess what? I found Grandma's hidden box of the Christmas letters. This is awesome. We've only had time to read one. Can't I stay and see the others?"

"We better not, Abby. The roads are getting a little slick, and I want to get home before they get too bad. You can come back tomorrow after school and help some more."

"Okay. Grandma, thanks, for letting me in on this treasure hunt. I can't wait to see the rest of them."

"See you tomorrow, Abs. Drive safely, Beth. Love you both."

After they left, Rose read slowly through each of the letters, alternating between tears and laughter. The memories hugged her while she prepared for bed. As she thanked God that she could still do her own transfer from wheelchair to bed, she also thanked Him for each experience the letters represented.

Over the next few days, Rose and Abby, and sometimes Beth, went through the letters, one by one. They drank lots of tea and shared many laughs and a few tears.

The second letter was written by Abby's Grandpa, who had died when Abby was just eight. Her memories of him were tender and powerful.

"This next letter is one that your grandpa wrote to our church family about his father." With that, Rose began to read and Abby listened, fascinated by the glimpse into a time before she was born:

December 1975

To Our Church Family,

I remember my earthly father with special affection at Christmas time. He was an exceptional man. His family was important to him and he never tired of expressing his love. On Christmas morning he was more like a brother than a father. His manner was that of youth; happiness flowed from him like a river, and excitement sparkled in his eyes. The wonder of Christmas never dimmed in his heart and neither did his faith in God. Please understand, he was not a saint. He was just a man, as frail and as vulnerable as any other man. But he was never alone, for he had discovered the source of all strength—Jesus Christ.

He used to say to me, when I was being troubled by one of childhood's many problems, "Dave, don't struggle alone. Tell me, and then we'll tell God. Between the three of us we should be able to work it out."

Today as a man looking back at another man, I realize his strength came from his sure knowledge of the presence of God in the world. He helped me to see that Christmas is much more than glitter. Christmas is the ultimate expression of love: God's love for us, our love for God, and our love for one another. That knowledge is the finest gift I ever received by my father's hand. It is the gift of love, life, and faith.

My dad died in 1960, but I can still feel his influence in my life. When I am down, I can still hear him say, "Dave, don't struggle alone. Tell God. He will hear, and He will help." We celebrate Christmas because God hears the voice of our need, and his answer is Jesus Christ.

Merry Christmas,
David
Rose
Karen
Beth
Chrissy

*****

"Wow, Grandma. He sounds awesome. I wish I could have known him... my great-grandfather."

"Me too, Abby. He died so long before I met your grandpa that I knew him only from the stories... and from this letter. I'm so grateful I kept it."

"What was it like for you to be the preacher's wife? Did you hate it? I can't imagine trying to live in a parsonage or trying to make your kids be holy."

Rose chuckled and said, "I don't think I ever expected the girls to be anything but normal kids. And most of the parsonages we lived in were very nice, and we had the chance to get to know and love so many wonderful people in the churches we served. But it wasn't always easy.

When Grandpa wrote that letter, we'd been in that first full-time appointment just a couple of years, but we stayed there for seven more.

Chrissy was just a month old when we started our time there; Beth was three, and Karen was five. It wasn't easy to pack up and leave after nine years, but the bishop said it was time. So we hugged those church folks we'd grown to love, cried a little, and off we went to the next parsonage.

Meanwhile, we'd bought this old farmstead for a get-away place. I hated it back then. It had orange carpet and green walls."

"Gross. Oops—sorry, Grandma. I didn't mean to interrupt."

Rose grinned and said, "It's okay, Abby. You're right. Those colors together were gross, indeed. And that wasn't the only reason I hated it back then. The heating, plumbing, and electrical systems were all shot. We spent our days off remodeling. We fixed things and made improvements through the years, but we found that the work actually became therapy for us. It was a good change of pace from our work at church. While we worked on the house, your grandpa often talked about growing up in both Erie and Oklahoma, where his father died.

After we retired, we had several wonderful years to enjoy it before your grandpa died. This is my home, and I love it. It's hard to leave, but I'll take the memories with me."

"Some of Grandpa's sermons had stories about that. I've read some of them after Mom posted them online. It's cool to think about all the people who loved him."

"You're right, Abby. But sometimes he had to preach even when he didn't feel well. This next letter was one I wrote after a Christmas Eve service when he was recovering from bronchitis." With that, Rose began to read, her voice tender with affection.

Christmas Day 1983

Sweetheart,

I love you! At times like this, I wish I could nurse you more professionally. The old corny cliché, "When you hurt, I hurt," is surprisingly accurate. Yet, there's sweetness in it somehow—a bonding beyond our early starry-eyed euphoria.

Whether you're serving Communion, putting tar on a roof, or cleaning a chicken coop, you're the most exciting man I know.

Please stay for a long, long time. Tonight the bit about your dad dying evoked a not-so-tiny lump in my throat for your loss. Thanks for making me aware of the preciousness of each moment, day, and year we've had and the gift of those still to come.

May they be many.

Sleep well, my carpenter.

I will always love you,
Me

*****

Just as Rose finished reading, Beth came in from loading boxes of books to be donated to the town library's book sale. She took her coat off, relaxed into a soft chair, peered into the box, and gasped.

"Mom," Beth asked, "is this next one the piece I wrote for school? I think I sort of remember doing it. I can't believe you kept it all these years."

"Yes, honey. This is your essay. Do you want to read it?"

"Sure. It'll be a blast from the past."

Beth reached into her purse for her reading glasses and began with a strong voice.

By the end of it, her words were soft, and her eyes flooded with tears.

Christmas 1984

The worst Christmas I ever had was when I was nine-years-old. Actually, it was the scariest. My mother was sick and had to be in the hospital by six o'clock

Christmas night. That same night I was up with my father crying because I thought Mom had gone there to die. I kept having all these horrible dreams that showed the hospital personnel cutting the wrong way, pulling out IVs, and just doing everything wrong. In the scariest dream, the hospital called to say my mother had passed away.

I was not allowed in the hospital room to see my mother and that led me to believe that they were keeping me away so they could harm her. She was there for four days and that fourth day, when she returned home, was the happiest day of my life.

*****

"Oh, Mom. I didn't realize or remember what this was about until I started reading it.

It brought it all back. I was so scared."

Rose sighed. "I was thirty-two-years-old and just glad to get it over with when I had that complete hysterectomy. I had no idea how frightened you girls were until I read your essay several years later. We can think we're protecting those we love by not talking about things, but maybe that's not always smart."

*****

"Where is everybody?"

"We're in here!" Rose, Abby, and Beth all called out at the same time, then they all laughed. Soon Beth's sisters, Karen and Chrissy, joined them.

"What are you three up to?" Karen asked. "I thought the packing would be almost done by now, and here you are just sitting around yakking, and, it looks like...crying too." Karen's smile cushioned her words, and Chrissy leaned over to give Rose a hug.

"How did you know I was wishing you were both here for this?" Rose looked at Abby suspiciously.

"Okay. I'm busted. I texted them, Gram, when I figured out this was getting to be a big deal. It didn't seem fair to leave Aunt Chrissy and Aunt Karen out of it. I told them all about your awesome box of Christmas letters and gave them the cliff notes on the ones we've already read."

Karen and Chrissy looked at each other then at Abby. Chrissy said, "I'm really glad you did, Kiddo. Mom, we brought supper. I put it in the oven, and it'll be ready in about an hour. Is that okay?"

"It's perfect," Rose said. "But before we read the next letter, I'll have to give all of you some family history that might be hard for you to hear. It'll be hard for me to share. But in case we don't have another chance like this all together without the men, I'd like to fill you in on some parts of my life that you lived through as children but that we haven't really talked about in years, if ever. And I think it'll be good for Abby to hear about it from me."

"How come, Grandma?"

"You're at the age when peer pressure will start throwing new temptations at you. Maybe my story will help you avoid a few bad decisions along the way."

Beth stretched out her legs from her spot on the sofa and said, "I think I know where this is going, and I guess you're right. Go ahead, Mom."

Rose looked at the gas log in the fireplace for a few seconds and then began.

"The summer before this letter was written I wrestled with my feelings about my mother's drinking. She wanted you girls to come to New York for a visit. I put off calling her until I finished with the gardening. Maybe I figured if I already hurt physically, it wouldn't hurt emotionally so much in case she wasn't quite sober. It didn't work; the call was awful. Part of me wanted to shriek, 'How can you think I'd trust you with any of my girls? Can't you see what you're doing to yourself? You're too drunk to remember any of this conversation anyway.' I lay on the bed in the dark and wept, 'Father, it hurts so much.'"

Rose paused, and her voice broke.

Chrissy got up and put her arms around her mother, helping to calm the moment.

Rose regained her composure and began again. "But you girls loved your grandparents and looked forward to spending time with your New York cousins, so I gave in and let you go. I think I told myself that certainly Mom wouldn't drink much with all of you there. Life is full of regrets, and that decision is one of mine.

"While you were gone, your dad and I tackled extra projects here at the farmhouse. We returned to the parsonage, tired and dirty. We'd been home just a little while when the phone rang, and your dad answered it. I could tell it was something serious when he sank onto the floor in the hall with the phone. I tried to guess what it was as I finished unpacking the truck. I heard him tell someone, 'Listen to Karen.'

"Finally he hung up and reached for me and said, 'It's bad. Your mother went berserk....' The details were horrible. Your dad held me, and God held us both.

"We showered and jumped back in the truck for the trip to New York. First we went to be with you girls. After I hugged you and convinced myself you were okay, I went to the hospital. I found Mom in both wrist and chest restraints. Apparently, she'd been on three different cold meds, all with 'Do not take with alcohol' warnings that she'd ignored. She was sing-songing numbers and names and then yelling at people who weren't there.

Her hallucinations grew more bizarre as the afternoon turned into evening.

"She ended up staying in the hospital for several weeks as they tested her for a variety of problems she didn't have. Finally they agreed with my diagnosis that beer plus cold meds equaled a kind of breakdown.

Our family intervention at the hospital took a toll on all of us. She was still on Librium and remembered little of that session, but it was a turning point. We all knew she needed help.

"It's only now after all these years that I can appreciate the amazing achievement of Mom's road to sobriety. She refused to do AA. She did agree to a series of out-patient counseling sessions with Uncle Charlie serving as her 'significant other' when none of the rest of us could handle that role. And she became a woman of prayer."

Abby said, "Gram, would you like a cup of tea before you go on? I can tell you're really shook up."

"Yes, honey. That would be wonderful."

While Abby left, the three daughters wiped their eyes and talked quietly among themselves, pulling up long-ago memories while Rose quietly praised God for His presence.

After Abby came back with the tea, Rose had a few sips of the piping hot, soothing liquid then began again with a stronger voice.

"I've often thought how much easier it would be if family drama points would space themselves out a bit instead of piling on top of each other with no manners at all. I shuttled myself back and forth between Pennsylvania and New York for the next few weeks. At the height of it during one phone call to your dad, he told me, 'I wasn't going to tell you yet, but things are pretty much under control now. Chrissy fell twenty feet out of a tree.' "

"Oh, my goodness, Mom," Chrissy said. "I haven't thought about that in so long."

"Apparently, you were pretty banged up and dazed, and they'd worried about a possible concussion. Mom was still a mess in New York, and I was really worried about my dad as he tried to cope with her condition, but I packed up and came back home with that all-too-familiar wishbone feeling.

"Let me tell you girls, your father was my rock of security through those crazy days. The next years went by in a haze of family and church events, and Grandpa and I had turns in and out of the hospital. I'm not sure what happened to some of the Christmas letters those years, but I'm glad I could still find this one that sort of sums up at least part of our love story. Chrissy, would you read this one, please?"

"Sure Mom."

Christmas 2000

Sweetheart,

After all these years, it should be easy to tell you how important you are to my happiness, but it's not. I am so prone to whine about needing time and space . It may not be so evident that as much as I need those, I need your constant presence in my life and in my heart more.

I watched you in the pulpit this morning and marveled, for the umpteenth time, at your ability to move people, to move me. You touch hearts and spirits and you challenge us to higher places in Christ.

Last summer there was a day we were in the grocery store and you went to get the milk. I snuck back to trade my favorite bread for yours, and you followed me with a grateful grin that made my day. Later, after you mowed with the hand mower and I had the cushy tractor detail, you let me use the last of the soft butter for toast. You pretended you'd rather have a baloney sandwich.

Both things were so little, but they meant a lot.

If I could, I'd wrap up in a pretty package:

- a gift certificate for every new tool you need/want

- and another for new clothes for both the office and the farm, things that would never be too tight or too loose so you wouldn't have to hike them up

- a real Plymouth Savoy-robin's egg blue...and a bunch of scale model tractors you don't have yet.

- oh, yeah--and a backhoe with a front-end loader.

Instead, all you get is this dumb letter from your adoring, admiring, faithful, if a bit messy, wife. Sometimes life's not fair. But other times it's pretty wonderful. You make each of my days very wonderful, indeed.

Love,
Rose

*****

Abby gave her grandmother a big hug. "You two sure were sappy but so sweet. I hope I can find somebody to love that much."

Just then the oven timer went off, and they all found their way into the kitchen. The talk around the table was full of love, laughter, and questions for Rose and for each other.

The sisters argued good-naturedly about who had been the most problematic child. Their gentle banter entertained Abby. It made her miss Megan, and she decided she'd make more of an effort to keep in touch with her big sister, the newlywed in Maryland.

After supper the girls cleaned up the kitchen, eventually all returning to the den where the letters waited.

Rose picked up the box, ready for another round. "The rest of these are a variety of silly, goofy, and sometimes corny letters. When I read them now, it's hard to believe that your dad survived three kinds of cancer over those years, yet he still he managed to make me laugh almost every day."

Abby said, "Grandma, can I read the next one?"

"Sure, sweetie. Here it is."

Christmas 2001

So, it's time for the Christmas letter again. Hard to believe how quickly the years roll around. Last year we took our children to visit our parents. Now, those children bring their children to us. Time is such a wonderful thing.

Thank God there are some things that time has not changed:
- We still don't listen to each other.
- We still look almost as good as we did last Tuesday.
- You still take way too many baths.
- I'm still not crazy about green food.
- Your children are strange, and mine are normal.
- I still love you and always will.

Anyway, you need some stuff, and I don't need this money. So take the money and get your stuff. I promise I won't come with you, and I'll like everything you buy. Even if it's a strange color. I love it when a plan comes together.

Speaking of plans . . . (you talk). Sorry about that. I needed a bathroom break.

Seriously though, I really like being married to you. You are thoughtful, kind, generous, and sort of understanding. You keep order at the church and make <u>all</u> the mistakes in the bulletins. I mean, could it be any better than that? What more can a man ask for?

Listen, if I had it all to do over again, I would ask for you again. Seriously!

I love you, Sweetie,
David

*****

Abby giggled and said, "I never realized that Grandpa was such a comedian. I love that bit about your kids and his kids since you just had these same three girls."

"He could be quite a card," Rose almost whispered with a catch in her voice.

Abby looked at her and said, "You really miss him don't you, Gram?"

"Every minute, every day. But I fight that sorrow by counting my blessings. Having you girls here to share these Christmas letters is a huge blessing right now. Who's reading the next one?"

Karen picked it up and said, "Hey, I remember this stationery. This must be the letter I wrote for your church newsletter."

Rose answered, "It is, indeed. Read it for us, honey."

Christmas 2003

Friends,

I have a challenge for you this year. And within that challenge is a part of my own

Christmas past. This is a small snapshot of my family and childhood that I hope will have meaning for you.

One of my most precious childhood Christmas memories is of helping my father with a task so small...in preparation for the most sacred moment of the year.

I was the oldest of three girls, and that allowed me the privilege of assisting my father with various 'preacher' jobs from time to time. Regularly, I considered myself the most fortunate daughter but never as much as on Christmas Eve.

On Christmas Eve I prepared the candles. We would leave early for the church, just my dad and me. I would be all dressed up, and he was the most handsome and dashing escort I could imagine. As we drove to the church, anticipation of the evening would well up in me until I felt as though I would burst with the joy. When we got to the church it was always quiet and dark and usually so cold I would keep my coat on for the first half hour.

But none of that mattered. All that mattered was the task bestowed upon me, the honor of being assigned to the candles.

It was a simple job. While Dad unpacked and cleaned old wax off the glass candleholders for the front of the church, I slipped new cardboard rings around smaller candles. Sometimes we talked, sometimes we sang. Sometimes we were just quiet and reflective.

We were always happy. There was always peace. We were wrapped in a sense of contentment that became much more elusive as I grew older.

So my challenge for you this year is to find a simple task and make it sacred. I don't literally help my dad with the candles anymore. I can't be there in person. But as the hour of the Christmas Eve service draws near, as I prepare myself for worship, he is with me. And I know as he still scrapes old wax off even older glass candleholders, I am with him. While we each hold a candle, watch the flame, and lend our voices to the song, there is peace, there is joy, and there is love.

Peace, Joy and Love to you this Christmas!

Karen

*****

Beth stood up and put her hand on Karen's shoulder. "Hey, Sis… that was pretty good.
I don't think I even read that at the time."

"No, back then you were more into shopping at the mall than reading the church newsletter."

Chrissy added, "What's new about that?"

Beth laughed and said, "Okay, okay, I deserve that. But it must be my turn. Can I read the next one, Mom? It looks like one of Dad's goofy poems, and I do remember those."

Rose smiled and said, "Sure, but before you do, maybe you should clue Abby in about Bob and Bobbie since they're in the poem."

"Bob and Bobbie? I never heard of anybody with those names in our family. Were they second-cousins-twice-removed or something?"

"No, silly," said Beth. "They were stuffed dogs that just sat around on furniture, but your grandpa would put a silly hat on one, and Grandma would put the other one someplace to surprise Grandpa. They acted like they were real dogs, and we teased Grandpa and Grandma all the time about how wacky that was." Karen and Chrissy looked at each other, agreeing with Beth.

"It may have seemed wacky to you girls, but for Grandpa and me, they were comic relief when pressures of the ministry got too heavy. Plus, they made very little mess and cost nothing to feed." Rose grinned as her daughters groaned in unison.

"One more thing, Abby. This will only make sense if you realize that by this time, your great-grandparents had died and I only had Aunt Dorothy left. Her last name is Berl. Okay, now you can go ahead, Beth."

"Whew… that was quite the intro. The back story is longer than the poem, but here goes."

Christmas 2006
>
> Hey, Creepy Guy,
>
> Only one night without that girl
> who's off with some aunt by the name of Berl
> Only one night of peace and quiet

(Unless Bob and Bobbie start a riot)
Only one night for me to stew
about all the things that trouble you:
Hernias, backache, a cold, and sore nose;
all of the things that just arose,
Only one night and I'll be back
to make sure things are all on track;
I'll brag of my guy with gifts of nine
So many things to make life fine,
Now go to sleep, no need to worry,
The Kia beast I shall not hurry
Enjoy your night and one more day
'til Creepy Girl comes back to stay.

Love always,
Rose

*****

Abby's laughter matched her mom's and both aunts' chuckles. "I can't believe you guys called each other 'Creepy Guy' and 'Creepy Girl,' Grandma. That's a riot."

"Actually, I can't either. It does seem pretty ridiculous now. I can't for the life of me recall how that got started. But at the time, there was no disrespect from either of us. It was just fun."

"Speaking of fun," Beth said, "who wants some popcorn?"

A female chorus of "We do!" filled the room.

"Okay," Rose said, "but after that let's just do one more letter tonight and save the rest for tomorrow."

"Sounds good, Mom," Chrissy said, adding, "I'll make the popcorn."

"And I'll help," Abby said.

Once they all settled with their snacks, Chrissy picked up the next letter and handed it to Karen. "You should read this one, Sis. It was from Dad to Lucy, and, after all, she's *your* daughter.

Karen took it tenderly and said, "I've never seen the actual letter, but I remember when Lucy called me about it. She and Peter had been transferred to North Dakota that summer. It was their first Christmas away from home. This letter meant a lot to her. Here goes."

December 19, 2010

Lucy,

It's been a long time since I saw you. A lot has changed in your life. You moved to the frozen northland, you bought a house, you learned to tear things apart and put them back together, you went back to school, you learned how to drive in real snow, and you found yourself with child. My guess is the baby is the big deal—right? I remember when your grandmother announced she was pregnant with your mother. I was only a little older than you are now.

When I got the news, I was very happy because that was how we had it planned. And then things just went along for, you know, about nine months, and at the end of it all your mom was born. So, this is the thing. I was totally unprepared for what I was going to feel when I first saw Karen. I could tell you that it's an unforgettable experience, but that would be the largest understatement of 2010. This is how it went for me when my first child was born:

1. I thought the time for the birth would never arrive. Don't worry; it always does.

2. When I saw your mother for the first time (hair matted to her head, face all wrinkled, crying, totally unhappy) I thought she was the most beautiful thing I ever saw.

3. I was speechless. That's a big problem for a preacher.

4. And then the reality that I was someone's father settled in, and I got scared. The being scared thing lasts a long time.

5. Finally, we all went home and started being a family. We are still doing that.

So, is this the way it will go for you and Pete?

I hope so. In fact, I envy you because what you are about to experience is some of the best life has to offer. Your life will soon be better, brighter, bigger, deeper, wider, and wilder than you have ever imagined.

Lucky you. Enjoy every moment....

I also remember when you were born. You were as beautiful as your mother was (is) and just as loud. And look at you now. All grown up, married, established in your own home, and about to be a mother.

It's not possible for me to be more proud of you. You will be a great mother. Your first child and those that follow will be in good hands.

And, just so you know, I can't wait to see my first great-grandchild.

> Merry Christmas
> Happy New Year
> See you soon.
> I love you, Lucy,
> Grandpa

Hi, Pete. Hope you are doing well.

*****

When Karen had finished, she wiped tears from her eyes. With every eye misty, they all hugged each other goodnight.

*****

Sunshine sparkled on the snow the next morning when Karen picked up her mother for church. When the rest of the family met them in the parking lot, they filed in and filled their usual pew. After the service, they went to lunch at their favorite restaurant where they made plans to meet later that afternoon to finish the letters. Rose knew she'd need to rest a bit first, so they set the time for three.

Laughter and excitement filled the air as they settled in the den for the Christmas letter finale. Rose began with a suggestion. "Since there are five letters left and five of us, how about if we just pass the box, and each one read the top one on the pile?"

"Sounds good to me, Grandma," Abby said. "Since I'm holding the box, and I see my name on the letter, I guess I'll go first."

Rose chuckled and said, "Sure, honey. That would be nice."

Abby held the letter carefully and said, "Hey! I was little when I wrote this. I sort of remember doing this." As she read, she only stopped twice to laugh at her younger self.

Christmas 2011

Dear Grandma,

I, your favorite grandchild (☺), made this weaving in art six weeks ago.

The colors represent the holiday colors for common holidays. I worked very hard on it, and hope you like it. I also wrote a poem.

WHAT I LIKE ABOUT YOU
What I like about you:
Your smile
Your cuddle
Your laugh
There are endless things
so I'll just say
What I like about you is <u>everything.</u>

Love you so much,
Abby

*****

Abby passed the box to her mother, who glanced down and said, "Looks like this was one Grandma wrote to Grandpa that same year."

Beth reached for the letter and smiled as she began.

6:11 a.m. Christmas morning 2011

Sweetheart,

Okay, Pilgrim. We survived another Christmas Eve, and by the time you read this, we'll both know what we wrapped up for each other.

But when I think of the consistent gift that you are in my life, I get misty. Bob gets so emotional, I have to threaten him with no TV for a week.

Day in and day out you keep me safe, keep me sane, drive me nuts, and impress the socks off me and then melt my heart.

Oops. Now you're stirring, so I suppose it's time to wipe the silly tears off and get ready to watch you peek around the corner.

Thanks for today and the last bunch of years, and the next....

All my love,
Your Rose

*****

"You two were better than Romeo and Juliet, Gram," Abby said. "Didn't you ever get mad at each other?"

"Sure we did, as all married couples do, but never for long. We learned early how to forgive each other and appreciate our differences."

The box, handed from Beth to Karen, was now very light. "I can't believe I get to read this one, Mom. I didn't even know you kept a copy."

Christmas 2011

Dear Karen,

We have come far. The memories we share of Christmases past in Erie, inHolcomb, in Grover, and so many other places. Each of them is precious, and each is full of His amazing power. You and Dad singing at Trout Run is such a special memory.

Mrs. Keiper looking at you in kindergarten was a prediction that you'd be a teacher someday. And so you were, and are, and more....

I only know the tip of the iceberg about what you handle on a regular basis, both in school and as a pastor's wife. Sometimes at my desk at church, I try to imagine you at work. I send up a silent prayer, and I'm so proud of you, whether or not I ever know or not what you're handling.

He knows. It's enough.

And you and Steve are on the great adventure of ministry that Dad and I have been on, but you're making your own way. You're dreaming your own dreams and obeying the voice of the Holy Spirit on your own terms. Your ministry is different from ours, and that's only right. But we all, the four of us, have each learned that apart from His strength, we're a mess. Sometimes, even with Him, we're a mess, and that's okay too. Our people need to see some of the messes so they can deal with their own without feeling inadequate.

So for this Christmas, the one after Dad's latest cancer scare and the one just before the second great-grandchild arrives, I am full of gratitude and hope.

I love you so, Karen,
Mom

*****

Now it was Chrissy's turn. She took the box, smiling at what she saw. The next letter was written on stationery she remembered. It had a pumpkin-colored border behind a goofy dog. Her mom knew orange was her favorite color.

Christmas 2011

Chrissy,

This guy must be a friend of Bob's. Actually, he was the only clip-art I could find with any orange on it, so he was the winner of your stationery contest ☺.

Maybe he has the winning ticket for an all-expense ticket to Palau—just right for a weary RN to get away for a week or two while the happy Grandma with the fake dog gets to babysit. I love dreaming up schemes that might make you smile.

I have a feeling that on a regular basis you are making many smiles possible on the job and at home. I think that happens even though you mostly feel like you don't have enough time or patience or strength to do any of it as well as you want to. We crazy Thomas women always seem to live in some kind of drama, and maybe that's part of what makes us so fascinating.

Ah, Chrissy, you have come so far. For all these years you've juggled school, work, and home. The challenges are huge, but you jump over each of them the way you used to jump hurdles in track: one at a time.

I have pictures in my mind of us on the beach at Palau, and in Montrose, and trips back and forth from New York, and so many more. Each is a jewel.

Love you so much,
Mom

*****

With one letter left, a letter everyone seemed to know had been written to Beth, the box was passed to Rose. Rose carefully picked up the letter, her voice strong as she began....

Christmas 2012

Dear Beth,

When you were little, you were, as you've heard me say so many times, the shy one.

Mrs. Keiper saw that first and rejoiced when the silence was lifted. That was the first of many hurdles you pushed past.

Others came one by one: boy traumas, moving so many times, the need to say good-bye to old friends, old houses, and then to fit into new neighborhoods, new schools.

Each time life handed you a challenge, you met it, not realizing that each one was God's stepping stone to teach you a little more about handling what would come. We often talk about Type 1 Diabetes as your biggest challenge and maybe it has been...or is. But it's just one more stepping stone for you.

You meet that challenge like all the others: with grace.

Now you're on a whole new path with a full-time, very challenging career that demands much from you. Beyond that, you are surrounded by three lively guys who fill your heart and your days.

I'm already looking forward to our spring retreat and to the chance to build new memories. We have so many wonderful ones already: Twila Paris moments, Treasure Lake, and more.

May 2012 bring you and yours blessings galore.

I love you so much, Beth,
Mom

*****

The box was empty, but the hearts of those present at such a special time were full of love and joy. The girls carefully placed each letter back in their proper order and handed the box to Rose. One by one, her daughters hugged her and tried to express what sharing the letters had meant to them. It was no use. The feelings went too deep. The memory they had just made would last a lifetime.

The sisters spoke quietly to each other as they gathered their coats and hugged Rose goodnight. Abby was last.

"Grandma, thanks for sharing the letters with us. Hearing about your life with Grandpa was awesome."

"It's been special for me too, honey. This has become a very special Christmas already."

Abby was almost at the door when she turned and gave her grandmother a big smile. "Grandma, thanks for giving me a really good idea. I think I know just what I'm doing for Christmas this year."

"And I can't wait to find out what it is," Rose said with a wink.

Made in the USA
Middletown, DE
17 October 2016